Lawyer Jory Dartmore runs across some confusing points in a case file. He calls the ex-employee who'd been working on the file, Attain Walsh, but his phone is picked up by the man's lover, Ssimeas. When Ssimeas tells Jory that Attain is unavailable for a while, he invites Jory to the ranch for dinner and to speak with Attain afterward. Jory accepts, curious about the man who'd won the heart of Attain, a confirmed bachelor.

Jory enjoys the meal and the company before slipping into an office to speak privately with Attain. When he opens the door to leave, he comes face to face with . . . something other. To Jory's eternal embarrassment, he faints.

Biscane would forever feel horrible for freaking out his mate, even though he wasn't trying to. He was just heading upstairs with his breakfast when a scent catches his attention. He can't resist pausing to sniff around the door. While growling with delight at the delicious aroma . . .the door opens, and Jory appears. Fortunately, Biscane's gargoyle reflexes and strength make it easy to catch him.

Upon finding out that Jory is a high-profile lawyer working at a firm with at least one homophobe, can Biscane figure out a way to bring his human round to the idea of sharing a life with him?

Playing with a Lawyer
Copyright © 2021 Charlie Richards
ISBN: 978-1-4874-3276-8
Cover art by Angela Waters

Published by eXtasy Books Inc or
Devine Destinies, an imprint of eXtasy Books Inc

Look for us online at:
www.eXtasybooks.com or www.devinedestinies.com

Playing with a Lawyer
A Paranormal's Love Book Thirty-Three

By

Charlie Richards

DEDICATION

Doesn't expecting the unexpected make the unexpected expected?
~Bob Dylan

CHAPTER ONE

Setting his reading glasses on his desk, Jory Dartmore sighed deeply. He leaned back in his chair, resting his head against the cushion behind him. Rubbing his eyes gently, he tried to make sense of what he was reading.

Except, the more Jory thought about it, the more he knew he was missing something.

The first meeting between the divorcing couple — Karl and Susan Riddle — had gone as expected. Susan had insisted on a larger cut of their estate than what their prenuptial agreement had outlined. Naturally, she'd claimed that was because Karl had cheated on her.

According to the notes made by Attain Walsh, the attorney who'd been handling the case at the time, he'd pointed out the three clauses that made that impossible without Karl's agreement. Of course, Karl had been adamant that he would never agree to that. Then the man had revealed that he had proof that Susan was having an affair, too.

God, why would anyone want to try for a committed relationship these days? There's just no way people can be trusted anymore.

Jory's thoughts returned him to Attain. The man had worked for their firm for years, following in his father's footsteps — George Walsh, one of their company's two other partners. Then Attain had hooked up with a guy at his best friend's ranch, George had revealed he was a homophobe, and Attain had quit the firm.

A confirmed bachelor choosing love over his job. Never thought I'd see that day.

1

Lowering his hands to his thighs, Jory refocused on Attain's notes. According to the data, the pair stopped squabbling, and the meeting ended fairly quickly after that. Jory didn't understand why, two weeks later, the woman was demanding the prenuptial agreement be voided.

What the hell happened?

Jory could think of only one person who would know, outside of the couple and Susan's lawyer, of course. No way in hell did he want to call the wife's lawyer to ask for his notes. Seeing as Jory didn't want to look ill-prepared or inept to Karl, his own client, asking the other lawyer would be a last resort. That meant he needed to find another way to verify his information.

With a frustrated growl, Jory picked up his cell phone. He found the contact he wanted and initiated the call. The line rang once, twice, three times. Just when Jory figured he would have to leave a message, a deep voice answered.

"Attain's phone. This is Ssimeas."

Arching one brow, Jory recovered quickly. "Hello, Ssimeas," he greeted. "This is Jory Dartmore. I used to work with Attain. Is he about?"

"Jory Dartmore," Ssimeas repeated slowly. "I recognize the name. Attain speaks highly of you and your abilities." After a second, he added, "And sorry, no. Attain isn't here right now. He's out moving cattle with Nicholas."

"Moving cattle?" Jory couldn't help but repeat that news. "Seriously?"

Ssimeas's deep chuckle sounded through the line. "Probably not what most people think of as fun, but it's Saturday afternoon, and my man gets a kick out of it."

Jory thought about that for a moment. "Huh," he murmured. "To each his own."

"Yup," Ssimeas immediately responded. From the sound of it, he was grinning. "Sounds like you could use a little down time, Jory."

2

"And why do you say that, Ssimeas?" Jory asked immediately, curious as to what made the man speak so brazenly. He couldn't remember the last time someone had done that. Normally, his high-powered lawyer persona caused people to defer to him. Attain's man obviously didn't react as most others.

Maybe that's how he snagged Attain's attention.

To Jory's amusement, Ssimeas laughed. "Well, it's pretty obvious," he claimed around his chuckles. "You're calling about work on a Saturday afternoon."

Jory scoffed softly, nodding even though he knew Ssimeas couldn't see it. Still, he felt compelled to ask, "How do you know I'm calling about work?"

After all, Jory hadn't told Ssimeas why he wanted to talk to Attain.

Ssimeas snorted, still sounding amused. "Have you ever called Attain before, Jory?"

"Fair enough," Jory replied with a grin of his own. "Will you tell Attain that I called, please? I have some questions about a case of his that I took over."

"I can do that," Ssimeas assured. Just as Jory was about to thank him and hang up, the man added, "Except, why don't you come here for dinner? It'll get you out of the house and away from work for a while. Then you can chat with Attain afterward."

"I — Uh, what?"

Jory couldn't remember the last time someone had shocked him, but Attain's man just had.

Ssimeas's warm chuckle came through the line. "Yup, you definitely need to get out more if that's your response to a simple dinner invitation."

Still too surprised to speak, Jory didn't respond to Ssimeas's teasing.

"Attain used to be that uptight, too," Ssimeas continued,

completely disregarding any propriety. "That's one of the reasons he would come out here to ride and play with the cows. Physical activity is a good stress relief." The sound of footsteps on wood came faintly through the line, telling Jory that Ssimeas was moving through his home. "So, come out tonight, Jory," he encouraged once more. "Fresh mountain air. Laid-back company. A couple of the guys are butchering a cow today, so the steaks will be fresh. Relax for the evening."

"Okay." The word was out of Jory's mouth before he could think better of it. Unwilling to second-guess himself—after all, it wasn't as if he had anything better planned for the evening—he asked, "Time and dress?"

With another low chuckle, Ssimeas told him, "The dress would be clothes, and the time is anytime after five but no later than seven or you might not get your favorite cut."

Smirking, Jory replied, "Then I better get there early. Can I bring anything?"

"Nope. Can't wait to meet ya, Jory."

To Jory's continued surprise, Ssimeas hung up without another word or waiting for him to respond. He shook his head as he placed his phone back on the desk. While he stared at the file open on his desk, he wasn't really seeing the words.

"What an interesting man," Jory commented as he thought about Ssimeas. Then he grinned and shook his head as he pulled up a different file. "Looking forward to meeting him, too."

For the next two hours, Jory slogged through another file that had landed on his desk due to a junior lawyer quitting. George's attitude had been getting progressively worse over the last six months. Ever since Attain had walked away from the firm and his father in favor of his lover, George had been taking out his anger on their people, and Jory had just had a meeting with Reginald that Friday in regards to what they could do about the situation.

They hadn't come up with a firm decision on how to approach the man, yet.

A glance at the time on his monitor told Jory it was already four-thirty. He transferred the files he needed to a flash drive, then shut down his laptop. Taking the drive with him, Jory headed out of his office and into his bedroom, placing it on his dresser.

Jory stripped out of his sweatpants and t-shirt and headed to the shower. As he quickly washed, he wondered what others would think of him if they knew his preferred clothing at home was soft and comfortable. As soon as he hit the door every evening, he stripped his suit and tie.

Good thing I rarely get unexpected visitors.

As Jory dried off, he realized Ssimeas was right about one thing.

Well, two things.

Jory working on Saturdays meant he had very little life, and he didn't have much in the way of hobbies.

As Jory pulled a pair of little-used jeans up his legs, he chuckled to himself.

Maybe I'll take up horseback riding. If it works for Attain . . .

While finishing dressing, Jory wondered if he could wrangle an invitation from someone at the ranch.

"Wrangle. Ha!" As soon as the words were out of his mouth, Jory rolled his eyes. "God, now I'm laughing at my thoughts and talking to myself. Not good. Time to get a life, Jory."

As Jory put the finishing touches on his outfit—a nice undershirt, a pullover sweater, socks, and dress boots—he wondered when his life had become so mundane. Moving through his penthouse condo, he peered around the space, taking in the high-end finishes and loft ceiling. He paused in the living room to stare out the French doors at the large veranda with its comfortable padded metal furniture, fire pit, and the magnificent view of the city, city park, and the river that divided it.

Right. My life became this when I allowed myself to become wrapped up in wealth.

Turning away from the stunning view, Jory headed to the front hall. He snagged a jacket, just in case the early spring evening grew cooler than he anticipated. Then he picked up his keys from the crystal candy dish on the small table beside the door and headed out of his condo.

Jory rode down the elevator to the underground parking garage of the seventeen-story building. Exiting the lift, he turned to the right, toward his assigned parking space. After hitting the key fob to unlock his *Lexus*, he climbed behind the wheel and began the drive to Nicholas Lindson's ranch.

Almost an hour later, Jory obeyed his vehicle's GPS prompt and turned onto a smoothly graveled driveway lined with fencing. He swept his gaze over the meadows broken by a smattering of trees here and there. Some of the cows seemed to be taking advantage of the shade, dozing beneath the bows.

As Jory drove by a few of the animals that were grazing close to the fence, he marveled at the idea that Attain had been herding the animals that afternoon. While he probably wouldn't admit it to anyone, he felt a little intimidated by the large beasts. Having grown up in the city, he hadn't been around live animals much.

His family hadn't even had a dog. His mother had been allergic. Instead, their family had had a large saltwater aquarium in the parlor, but it had been a showpiece, so guests could see his father's wealth.

Parking in front of a large ranch house, Jory shut off the engine. He hesitated, suddenly wondering if Ssimeas had the authority to invite guests.

Does Lindson know I'm coming? Does Attain? Guess I should have worried about that before now.

Grabbing his phone, Jory intended to call Attain's line again. Before he could even wake the device, the front door of the home opened and several men exited. He recognized Attain immediately, although he'd never seen him in jeans, a flannel shirt, and cowboy boots. Between that and the huge grin on his face, Jory decided Attain's lifestyle change looked good on him.

Jory recognized Nicholas Lindson, the owner of the ranch, from the news. There'd been a scandal involving his family. Evidently, the man Nicholas knew as his father — Baltus — was actually his uncle. Baltus's younger brother, Albert, was his real father. That came out after Albert returned to the ranch with a male lover in tow, setting off the vengeful wrath of Nicholas's mother, Katrina.

There's probably more to that story, but it's not my place to ask.

As Jory eased from his vehicle, he took in the two men standing with Attain and Nicholas. They were, in a word, huge. The older-looking man with long, steel-gray hair who had his arm slung around Nicholas's shoulders had to stand over six and a half feet. The grinning, dark-featured male holding Attain's hip possessively was only a couple of inches shorter.

Jory had never considered his six-foot-one-inch frame small, but next to those guys . . . he did. Working out regularly, he kept himself in shape, but the men here were built like linebackers. He wondered briefly at the size of the horses they must need to carry someone their size.

Bet they have to ride draft horses.

Doing his best to hide his intimidation, Jory pasted on a smile and started toward the porch steps.

Attain greeted him with a grin. "Hey, Jory. It's good to see you again." He held out his hand, and the pair shook. Chuckling, Attain added, "I know you joining us has to be partly related to something from the firm, but Ssimeas coulda knocked me over with a feather when he told me you were coming."

Jory winced as he nodded. "Sorry. I hope it's okay."

"Of course, it's okay," Attain immediately replied. He waved toward Nicholas. "This is Nicholas Lindson, but you probably already knew that."

Nodding, Jory shook hands with the ranch owner. "I did, but it's nice to officially meet you." After releasing the man's work-roughened hand, he waved to indicate the area. "Your ranch is stunning."

"Good to meet you, too," Nicholas replied. With a wide smile, he swept his gaze over his spread. "Thanks. We surely do like it out here."

"I don't blame you," Jory replied. After a second, he added, "Thank you for letting me crash your barbeque."

"The more, the merrier," Nicholas replied. Then he indicated the man next to him. "This is my fiancé, Bodb."

Jory offered his hand. "Nice to meet you."

As the huge guy offered, "Same to you," and reached for his hand, Jory wondered if he would squeeze too tight in some kind of pissing contest. To his pleasant surprise, he didn't. His small smile appeared genuine, the corners of his eyes crinkling.

After letting go of Bodb's hand, the other big man held out his. "And I'm Ssimeas." With a wink, he added, "But you probably knew that already, too."

"I kinda figured," Jory replied with a grin. "What with you having that possessive hand on Attain's hip and all."

Ssimeas laughed heartily. "Guilty as charged. Can't help how much I love holdin' my man here." Then he leaned down and pressed his lips to Attain's.

Jory had never seen two men make out, and he felt an odd flutter in his gut. Even his groin warmed a little at the fierce display of propriety.

Nicholas chuckled as he patted Jory on his shoulder.

"Come on, Jory," he urged. "I'll show you around back while Ssimeas finishes ravishing Attain."

Jory nodded and followed, striding along the porch decking beside the other man.

"You'll have to forgive Ssimeas," Bodb added from Nicholas's other side. "He hasn't seen Attain much this afternoon, so he's feeling a need to reconnect with his lover."

"Sure, sure," Jory immediately replied. "I'd never tell another how to behave toward their significant other in their own home."

Bodb nodded as he peered over Nicholas's head at him. "Just wanted to be sure we weren't making you uncomfortable."

Jory shook his head, fighting the heat threatening his cheeks as he admitted, "Not that kind of uncomfortable."

"Aahhhh," Bodb murmured.

Nicholas clapped him on the back once more, saying, "Well, come on around back. You'll have plenty of eye-candy here, and no one will be offended if you stare." With a wink, he continued, "Just no touching without permission."

"Uh, n-no, of course not," Jory stuttered, embarrassed as hell at the implications of their words.

Before Jory could say more, they rounded the last corner of the house and a sprawling, two-tiered deck stretched out before him. Many more men, and even a few women, milled around the space, and the fragrant scent of grilling meat perfumed the air. Jory's stomach rumbled.

With a smile, Nicholas guided him toward a group of people, and another round of introductions ensued.

CHAPTER TWO

L ike a light switch had been flipped, Biscane came awake from roost. He peered around the hay loft, not at all surprised to find himself alone. As the only unmated gargoyle on the ranch, he was the only one forced to roost at every sunrise. All the others could choose when they would sleep as a stone statue — a gargoyles' version of REM sleep — as long as they did it for several hours at least once a week.

Biscane rose to his feet and stretched his arms over his head and his wings to either side. He couldn't touch the twenty-foot high ceiling, but his wings brushed against the hay bales on either side of him. Nicholas had set up a secluded nook in the hay loft. While it wasn't large, it did give them a safe place to roost.

His stomach rumbled, and he lowered his arms. Even over the scent of horse, manure, hay, and leather, he could smell the scents of grilled meat. He recalled Stanley Redfeather — the Native American foreman of the ranch — telling him that they planned to butcher a cow that morning.

Evidently, the cow had rejected her calf, refusing to allow it to nurse. The cute little fellow was in a stall below and being raised by hand. Due to the fact that she'd done the same thing to her prior calf, they'd decided to butcher her instead. While it might seem harsh, in the cattle business, if she wasn't going to raise her calves, then she would be put to another use — feeding the ranch hands.

Hoping one of the other gargoyles had put aside some

heart and liver for him, Biscane headed toward the loft's double doors. His mouth watered just thinking about fresh-grilled heart. He'd seen a number of the ranch hands look askance at him and his fellow gargoyles the first time they'd given it to Pauline. She was a red fox shifter mated to another gargoyle enforcer — Lebone — and worked as the ranch's cook. She hadn't batted an eye at their request.

Biscane eased open the loft door and peered around the area. Spotting a vehicle he didn't recognize parked in front of the house, he realized he'd forgotten his phone. He returned to the roosting area and pulled it from the charger where he'd left it the morning before.

Seeing several texts, Biscane scrolled through them. One was a notice of who he would be working with that evening — Sindrid and Lludd. As the only unmated gargoyle, Biscane naturally took the full night shift. The other mated enforcers broke up the duties and rotated them. That way they would have plenty of day hours to spend with their mates.

Doing his best to quell the jealousy caused by the fact that he hadn't yet found his mate, Biscane moved to the next text. That one was from Lebone, letting him know Pauline had set aside some heart and liver for him, and his plate was being kept warm in the oven. He grinned, appreciating her thoughtfulness.

The third message was from Elder Bodb and told Biscane who the driver of the car was — an unknowledgeable human there to see Attain. He was warned to be careful as he flew to the bunkhouse to get cleaned up. Then Bodb ordered him to use a side door when making his way to his office to go over reports before starting his shift.

Biscane slipped out of the loft, stepping into air. Stretching his wings, he caught himself. After closing the second-story loft door, he zipped to the bunkhouse. He headed inside and immediately spotted LeeAnn sitting at the table playing cards

11

with a couple of other hands. She grinned at him and put down her cards as she rose from the table.

Knowing LeeAnn's intent—to ask if he needed help in the shower—Biscane tried not to give her the chance. He'd slept with her a few times several months before, and she'd quickly become clingy. Ssimeas had warned him that she was angling for a boyfriend. Biscane wished he'd listened to the male and never gone back for seconds.

The human female wasn't his mate, and she knew it.

So why does she continue to pester me, then?

"How was the barbeque?" Biscane asked loudly as he hurried toward the stairs that led to the second floor. There was an empty bedroom up there, so there was a good chance that the jack-and-jill bathroom it shared with a second bedroom would be empty, too. He also knew fresh loincloths were stored there.

"Fresh steak is never bad when Lebone is doing the grilling," Stanley called back. His dark-eyed gaze flicked to LeeAnn, to Biscane's face, then back again. Obviously missing nothing, he narrowed his eyes as he focused on the female wrangler. "I saw Pauline set a plate aside for ya. You headed over there, Biscane?"

"I am," Biscane confirmed. "Can't wait. It smells amazing outside."

Biscane knew that while Pauline did the cooking and baking, her gargoyle mate did the grilling.

"Just gonna get cleaned up real quick," Biscane continued. "Then I'm gonna take that plate up to Bodb's office. He texted me about a report he wants to go over."

"Have a good night then," Stanley encouraged before saying, "Are you gonna finish this hand with us, LeeAnn?"

LeeAnn flashed a smile over her shoulder. "Maybe. Just a sec." Even as Stanley narrowed his eyes, the woman refocused on Biscane, resting a hand on his forearm. "I was just about to take a shower, too. Wanna conserve water with me?"

Even though Biscane's half-softened morning wood would have happily taken LeeAnn up on that, he knew he couldn't. She was still too clingy even after he'd told her no on several occasions for the last three months. Biscane had to stick with his right hand until she moved on.

Gods, I hope she moves on soon.

"No, LeeAnn," Biscane replied softly, easing away from her. "I need to get to that meeting with Elder Bodb. I don't want to keep him waiting."

"Oh. Of course." While LeeAnn scented of disappoint-ment—as well as a little annoyance—she kept a soft, inviting smile curving her lips. "Then we'll do it another time."

Before Biscane could counter her statement, LeeAnn turned and headed back to the table, swishing her hips seduc-tively. He ignored the way his blood began to pump south and turned away from her. Out of the corner of his eye, he spotted the concern on Stanley's Native American features for just a second before the foreman cleared the expression.

Biscane hustled upstairs, feeling the exact same way.

When will LeeAnn learn and leave me alone?

Thinking with his dick had never been a fault of Biscane in the past, so he couldn't figure out how he'd fallen into that trap with LeeAnn. He'd known that fucking with someone on the ranch where he lived was a bad idea. Still, she'd been per-sistent, and he'd been horny.

Now look where that got me.

Still horny, fighting my desire for a woman I don't actually want, and annoyed at her continued advances, which just seems to make everything worse.

Fighting back a growl under his breath, Biscane reached the bedroom he wanted. He dropped his dirty loincloth in the appropriate basket, then hopped into the shower. As he soaped up his body and enjoyed the heat of the spray, he peered down at his half-hard prick.

Biscane shook his head. The second he'd been out of sight

of LeeAnn, he'd immediately softened. His thoughts of her helped, too, so he was damn confounded as to why *seeing* her brought on such a rush of arousal.

While Biscane had never and would never consider himself a coward, he decided discretion was the better part of valor. After drying off and donning a new loincloth, he headed out of the bunkhouse — via the second-story window. Biscane easily floated to the ground before wrapping his wings around himself and heading to the main house.

As Biscane had been instructed, he headed in through a side door close to the kitchen. The scent of food caused his stomach to growl once more. Humming appreciatively, he sought out the source.

Pauline was still in the kitchen, tidying up with the help of her gargoyle mate, Lebone.

"Evening, Pauline, Lebone," Biscane greeted, smiling at the pair. "It sure smells amazing in here."

"Good evening, Biscane," Pauline replied with a bright grin. "I have something squirreled away just for you."

While Pauline had been speaking, Lebone had nodded and murmured his hello. Then he turned an indulgent and loving smile on his mate as she headed to the oven. When Pauline bent to open the oven door and pull out the wrapped platter, Biscane saw the lust flair in Lebone's eyes.

Biscane quickly averted his gaze as jealousy again soured his gut. As happy as he was for everyone at the ranch who'd found their bond — and that was every other paranormal except himself — he wanted that desperately. Biscane didn't know what he'd done to have Fate forsake him so.

Swallowing hard, Biscane focused on the food. He knew those thoughts weren't productive. Instead, he needed to have faith that Fate would bring him his mate when the time was right.

Gods, I hope that's soon.

Except, if I find my mate, what will LeeAnn do? She's turned

14

damn clingy. Surely she wouldn't cause problems, would she? After all, she knows about mates.

Of course, if Fate doesn't bring my mate for another thirty years, LeeAnn's clinginess would be a moot point because she would most likely be dead or have moved on to another job by then.

Damn, I hope I'm not waiting another thirty years.

Biscane wasn't certain if he could go on watching everyone in mated bliss for that long.

"Hey. Everything okay?"

Hearing Lebone's deep voice and feeling his hand on his shoulder yanked Biscane out of his thoughts. He forced a crooked smile as he nodded. "Yeah. Fine. Just lost in thought." Biscane reached for the plate Pauline was holding out to him, pulling away from the other gargoyle.

"Not good thoughts, I'd wager," Lebone commented astutely.

Biscane scoffed as he took the napkin roll, which held his silverware. Heading toward the kitchen's exit, he claimed, "Just need a cup of coffee."

As Biscane moved through the huge dining room to the side board that held the ever-full coffee carafes, he glanced at the open pass-through where plastic tubs rested. Once done eating, everyone would put their dishes into them, and Pauline would collect them for washing. He didn't miss the worried looks the pair exchanged.

Ignoring them, Biscane placed his platter and silverware down in favor of grabbing a large mug and a carafe of dark roast. Just as he was about to pour, a scent tickled his senses. He paused, tipped his head back, and flicked out his tongue. Inhaling deeply, he used the hundreds of extra sensory receptors on his tongue to parse out the interesting aroma.

Biscane hummed appreciatively as the flavors of something masculine filled his senses. Placing the mug and carafe down, he turned, but the room was empty. Interested in locating the source, he inhaled again, then chose a direction.

Heading for a hallway to the left, which held an office and a library, Biscane ignored Lebone calling his name. He tracked the delicious smell to a closed door. Leaning forward, he pressed his nose against the crack and drew in a deep lungful.

Whoever was inside smelled *divine*. His cock thickened quickly, and his blood heated in his veins. He felt the distinctive urge to find the source and rub himself all over him.

Holy shit! My mate is in there.

The realization caused a rumble of delight to burst from his chest and a grin to curve his lips.

At long last!

Just as Biscane heard Lebone call a warning, the door in front of him opened. The human before him stumbled backward a step as his deep brown eyes widened. The scent of shock mixed with a hint of fear flooded the air.

Then the muscular human's eyes rolled to the back of his head, and he began to drop.

Biscane lunged forward, and he swept the man destined to be his mate into his arms. Peering at the human he cradled, he gloried in the fact that finally, after so many centuries of waiting, Fate had brought him *the one*. She hadn't forgotten him after all.

Sweeping his gaze over him, Biscane admired the man's muscular lines, not at all hidden beneath his sweater and jeans. The touch of gray at the temples of his dark-brown hair coupled with his aristocratic features gave him a distinguished look. His long lashes graced his cheeks, and Biscane wished for them to flutter open so he could once again see the man's beautiful brown eyes.

"Biscane," Lebone snapped, finally cutting through his admiration of the man he held. "What the hell? Put Jory on the sofa." He thrust a tanned hand through his hair and frowned at Biscane. "We have some damage control to do now."

Growling, Biscane glared at Lebone as he clutched his human — Jory — tighter to his chest. "Mine," he snarled. "Never giving him up."

Lebone's eyes widened as he cocked his head. He even lifted his hands in placation. "Okay." Still focusing on Biscane, he turned his head a little and spoke to the other occupant of the room, whom Biscane had barely noticed. "Attain, run upstairs and get Bodb. We have a situation here."

Attain nodded and scurried around them, vacating the room.

Lowering his hands, Lebone asked, "So, uh . . . you think Jory is your mate, huh?" He pointed at the human in Biscane's arms. "That's Jory Dartmore, by the way. A lawyer who works at the same firm where Attain used to."

What Jory did for a living was of little consequence in Biscane's mind. The human was his mate, so he would make it work. The gift of his full name was appreciated, though. It meant Biscane would be able to research him.

"Yes, Jory is my mate." Biscane couldn't keep the pride from his tone as he spoke those life-altering words. "Mine."

"Oh, you have *got* to be kidding me," LeeAnn snapped, announcing her presence in the doorway. "No way is that guy your mate. Not after everything I went through to make you mine."

Biscane's instincts screamed at him to get Jory away from the woman who was attempting to counter his claim.

Even as Lebone stated, "LeeAnn, what are you talking about? You know we don't choose our mates," Biscane ignored them. He rushed across the room and flung open the French doors leading to the front porch. Spreading his wings, he took to the sky.

Irrational or not, Biscane had to get away from those who would try to take his mate away from him. His senses screamed that something was wrong. He needed his human in a safe place.

Turning in the direction of the barn, Biscane flew to the one place that represented safety to him—a safe place to roost—the barn's loft.

CHAPTER THREE

Jory slowly swam to wakefulness, trying to figure out why his brain felt so sluggish.

What happened?

Recalling spending Saturday evening with Attain and those at the ranch, Jory almost began to smile. Except, he didn't think he'd drank that much, but his head sure pounded as if he had. He also realized he wasn't in his own bed.

And there's an arm wrapped around my waist.

What the fuck?

Jory didn't remember meeting anyone who'd sparked his interest, and he sure wouldn't indulge in a one-night stand at Nicholas's ranch.

Talk about bad form.

"Relax," a deep voice rumbled from behind him. "You're okay. Just take a few cleansing breaths. I'll keep you safe."

For a second, Jory froze as shock flooded him. *Holy shit. I'm in bed with some guy.* Then he forced himself to obey the man. After all, what else was he supposed to do?

To Jory's surprise, he found the earthy scent of the man holding him . . . amazing. He felt arousal begin to burn through his veins. His blood started to flow to his dick, causing him to plump more swiftly than he had in years.

Okaaaaay . . . maybe that's why I decided to climb into bed with this guy.

Except, then Jory realized he still had his clothes on. Had they passed out before they could do anything? That would have been damn embarrassing.

How can I ask what happened without sounding like an idiot?

"My name's Biscane," the man behind him whispered into his ear while rubbing his hand over Jory's chest. "I understand your name is Jory Dartmore and that you're a friend of Attain's?"

"Yes," Jory replied, parsing out the meaning of those words. If he hadn't even gotten the man's name, why would he have gone to bed with him? Finally opening his eyes, he frowned. Some of the other scents—beside Biscane's very alluring cologne—registered. *And isn't that an odd name?* "Why are we surrounded by hay bales?"

Jory took in his surroundings. The hay was stacked six high all around them. The bed they lay on was low to the planking floor. While a nice dark-blue sheet lay above and below them, Jory could still feel that they had to be lying on some kind of cot or futon.

"Are we in a hay loft?" Jory blurted out the odd idea, even as he couldn't think of another solution to what his brain was telling him.

"We are," Biscane confirmed easily. "I needed to get you somewhere safe."

"Safe?" Confused, Jory began turning his head. "What do you mean?"

A dark hand slipped over Jory's eyes, blocking his view. "Please don't turn yet, Jory." There was a definite hint of worry in Biscane's deep voice. "There are some things I need to explain first."

Licking his lips nervously, which resulted in sliding his tongue against Biscane's flesh, Jory practically groaned upon tasting the man. He barely resisted the urge to do it a second time. Swallowing hard, he urged moisture down his suddenly too-dry throat.

Damn. When was the last time that happened to me?

Once Jory could speak, he murmured, "Okay. What's going on?"

If the man holding him could share reservations, he figured it was safe for him to do so as well.

Jory felt something soft nuzzle against the back of his neck, causing the hairs there to stand on end. Chills traveled down his spine even as he guessed it was the other man's lips. The fact that then Biscane kissed the skin there before speaking was a dead giveaway, too.

"There is more going on at this ranch than one would think at first glance," Biscane began, his words a little halting. "The people here . . . there's more to them than what meets the eye."

Unable to help himself, Jory teased, "You mean, they're *Transformers*?"

Biscane paused for so long that Jory worried he'd insulted the man. He was about to apologize when the guy behind him claimed, "We do transform, yes. Do you already know of the paranormal?"

Jory immediately realized that they were talking about two entirely different things. "Paranormal," he repeated slowly, thinking quickly. As a lawyer, he was paid for his quick mind to find solutions while in court. The skill helped right then, too. "Do you mean things that are not of this plane? Um, ghosts or specters. Demons and angels?"

While Jory would never consider himself a religious man, he'd spent a summer in New Orleans with his aunt and uncle — on his mother's side — when his parents were going through a divorce. It had been an eye-opening experience, and he firmly believed that magick and voodoo existed.

"Mmmm, not exactly."

The fact that Biscane didn't immediately counter his comment about ghosts, angels, and demons told Jory so very much. The man behind him obviously believed in them, too.

Interesting.

"So, what paranormal are you talking about?" Jory asked curiously.

"Gargoyles, shifters, and vampires."

Jory gaped upon hearing those words. Biscane said them so matter-of-factly.

Well, if a guy believes in other things, why not them, too?

"Uh, I didn't realize those were actually real, too," Jory admitted slowly before musing, "But I suppose the stories have to come from somewhere."

"Exactly." The relief filling Biscane's tone was damn near palpable. "But seeing us for the first time is always a shock, so I can understand why you fainted."

"Wait." Furrowing his brows behind the guy's hand, Jory asked, "I fainted? When the hell did I do that?"

Suddenly, Jory recalled being in the office with Attain. He'd been discussing a case with the other man. After showing him the files, Attain had pointed out where things had been deleted, purposefully sabotaging the case notes. Then Attain had emailed Jory a copy of the originals from his own laptop.

Good thing the man had kept backups, even if he had apologized and said he'd intended to delete them.

"There was a creature at the door," Jory blurted out, recalling the huge, hulking black beast that had been growling at the office door. "What happened to it?"

Biscane sighed deeply. "That creature at the door is called a gargoyle," he murmured, his voice suddenly sounding strained. "And . . . I'm right here, holding you, hoping you'll accept me."

"What?" Jory cried, shock flooding him. Jolting, he turned his head as he half-twisted on the cot. "Holy shit!"

Jory jerked to a sitting position as he took in the beast that lay sprawled next to him, the one that had been holding him in his arms . . . which had felt so very nice. Even as his mind acknowledged that fact, disbelief tried to needle into his brain. There had to be a logical explanation for why he thought he was seeing the winged creature lying there.

Having never done drugs in his life — hell, he even avoided them when he was injured or sick — he knew *that* wasn't the cause. He took taking care of his body seriously. His brain was his money-maker, and poisoning it was counter-productive.

"Okay, think, Jory Dartmore," Jory murmured to himself as he stared down at . . . Biscane. "So, you're really seeing what you think you're seeing, no matter how crazy it seems."

Jory realized he was talking to himself again, but under the circumstances, he decided it was okay.

"I've seen a demon, so this isn't so different," Jory whispered. "Although, it had no interest in holding me."

That he knew of, anyway. It had looked at him with black, soulless-looking eyes, then turned and headed in the other direction, disappearing between mangrove trees.

"When did you see a demon?" the creature — gargoyle — Biscane — asked, sounding a mixture of curious and concerned. "And I would never hurt you, Jory. *Never*."

Nodding slowly, Jory accepted that. After all, he'd been lying with the male, and since Jory had pushed down the sheet when he'd bolted upright, it was so very obvious to see that the gargoyle *was* a male. The loincloth it wore gave that fact away.

And damn, is he well-endowed.

A very impressive erection tented the fabric.

Feeling a big hand cradle his neck jolted Jory out of his perusal of the broad and muscled male form beside him. Feeling the pressure of a thumb under his chin urged him to lift his gaze to Biscane's face. His thick lips were curved in a hint of a smile, and the male's black eyes were like liquid pools of desire.

"Good god," Jory whispered, unable to do anything but voice his thoughts. "You want me. Like . . . like want me like . . . *that*."

Jory would have rolled his eyes at how inane he sounded

if he'd been able to tear his gaze away from Biscane's intense one.

"Yes, Jory," Biscane whispered huskily. "I do want you like . . . *that*."

It took every bit of self-control Jory possessed to make his mouth work. "I, uh . . . why?"

Biscane blinked once, twice, then seemed to shake himself out of whatever he'd been thinking about.

Considering the way the heated desire eased from Biscane's square-jawed features, Jory could guess at what he'd been thinking. His tone had given him away, too. Still, as much as Jory was damn tempted to see just how good a lover the gargoyle was, he knew that wasn't what he should be focusing on right then.

"Paranormals have something called a mate," Biscane replied slowly. "A soul mate, someone to bond with. Someone who completes them."

Jory couldn't hide his confusion as he furrowed his brows.

With a smile that could only be called *beyond satisfied*, Biscane swept his gaze over Jory's frame. "That's you, Jory. You are my soul mate." His voice lowered to a soft whisper as he added, "And I have been searching for you for such a very long time."

Cocking his head, Jory struggled to process that one. "I—" He cleared his throat before ever-so-eloquently asked, "What?"

Biscane sighed deeply, his smile softening to an expression of understanding. "This is a lot for most humans to take in," he commented. "Especially if they don't know anything about paranormals and mating or bonding to begin with."

When Biscane released Jory's chin only to tease his fingertip along his eyebrow and over to the hair at his temple, he thought he should have felt the urge to jerk away. Instead, he didn't. For some reason, he wanted to turn his head and nuzzle into his gentle touch.

Jory had never experienced anything like that before, which worked him up a little. Easing back a bit on the cot, he put a few inches between them. That was about the time he realized it wasn't just a sheet draped over his legs. Biscane had one huge black wing over his thighs and lower legs, too.

With his focus snagged on the appendage, Jory couldn't help but reach out. He rested his fingertips on it and lightly skimmed along it. The skin felt deceptively soft—like high-end leather.

A low moan, a sound like it had been ripped from someone's throat, filled the room.

Snapping his gaze from Biscane's wing, Jory jerked his attention to the male's face. He parted his lips in surprise when he saw the expression on the gargoyle's face. There could only be one way to describe it—pleasure-pain of the highest order.

"B-Biscane?" Jory stammered, confusion flooding him anew. "What?"

Biscane inhaled deeply, his nostrils flaring. When he lifted a hand, it trembled. Gently, he placed it on Jory's upper arm.

"There is so much to explain, my mate," Biscane murmured in a rough voice. "First, a gargoyle's wings are sensitive. A touch to them can cause great pleasure, leaving us nearly writhing with ecstasy." After clearing his throat, Biscane rumbled, "So most gargoyles will only ever allow their mate to take such a liberty." His voice lowered to a husky whisper. "Myself included."

Jory stared at the gargoyle in shock. "Y-You've never allowed another to t-touch your wings?"

"Not like how you just did," Biscane told him.

Cocking his head, Jory asked, "What do you mean?"

"Soft strokes of appreciation," Biscane answered, finally easing to a sitting position beside him. "Not an accidental touch as people pass in the hall or jostle together in a room." Resting his free hand on Jory's leg, he added, "Or in battle as a weapon."

"Oh," Jory murmured, trying to catch his suddenly short breath. "Um, okay."

Battle?

The idea of fighting jarred Jory's memory. "You said earlier that I was in danger."

Biscane tipped his head to the side a little, and he appeared to be in thought. "I did?"

He did, right?

Jory needed to gather his wits, and Biscane's hands on him were definitely making it difficult.

Especially how high up his hand is on my thigh.

His cock was very, *very* interested in that.

Shoving his arousal to the back of his mind, Jory rested one hand over Biscane's on his thigh. He squeezed, keeping it in place so it couldn't move anymore. With his second hand, he grabbed Biscane's other wrist.

With surprising ease, Jory pushed Biscane's hand away from him. Considering the muscles on the male—he practically looked like a bodybuilder—he knew the gargoyle was ceding control to him. Jory spotted the look of hurt on Biscane's face, and he realized the guy was getting the wrong idea.

Uh, what idea is that?

The unexpected expression on the gargoyle caused Jory's brain to stall. "What's wrong?" he asked, turning his hand so he could grip the gargoyle's thick fingers. "Are you okay?"

Biscane glanced from where Jory held his hand before returning his focus to his face. "You pushed my hand away," he began slowly, betraying his confusion. "You're not rejecting me?"

Jory realized then that they'd gotten so far off track that he wasn't even certain what they were talking about anymore.

"Uh . . . I really don't know what that means, Biscane," he admitted. "Rejecting you for what?" Glancing at where Biscane touched his thigh before meeting his gaze again, Jory guessed, "Rejecting you as a sexual partner?" Before the male could answer, he quickly added, "I've never been with a guy before, but I'll admit I'm attracted to you. I'll, uh . . . just need a little time to figure it out."

"That's only part of it, Jory."

Hearing Attain's softly spoken comment, Jory glanced around.

Before he could see the man, Biscane wrapped not only his arms around him, hauling him close, but his wings as well. On top of that, a low rumbling growl sounded from his chest.

Instead of fearing Biscane, Jory had the distinct impression that the gargoyle was trying to keep him safe. He just didn't understand why . . . or from whom.

"What's going on, Biscane?" Jory asked softly, relaxing against his side in hopes the move would help calm the male. "You know Attain would never hurt me."

"I know," Biscane answered a little too quickly. The thick ridges over his eyes — ones that reminded Jory of eyebrows — drew together. "Just . . . I need to keep you safe, and something is wrong."

"Talk to me, Biscane." Bodb crouched on top of the hay bales to Jory's left. "What has set you off, old friend?"

Biscane's hold seemed to relax just a little upon seeing the man, even though he didn't release Jory.

"I'm not certain, Elder."

Elder?

Chapter Four

Biscane scented Jory's confusion. The slightly bitter smell filled the small space. He knew he hadn't been explaining things well, and he appreciated his elder's arrival, knowing the other male would help.

Still, he couldn't escape the nagging feeling that his mate was in danger.

Finally, it clicked.

"I think LeeAnn is going to cause trouble," Biscane blurted out.

"But she knew you weren't mates, right?" Elder Bodb glanced from Biscane to Jory before pinning a questioning gaze on him. "You didn't lead her on."

"No, Elder," Biscane assured. "Never." As much as he hated discussing his past in front of Jory before they'd even started their bond — hell, before his human even understood what was between them — he had to try to explain his paranoia to his elder. "I discontinued that dalliance months ago, but she's having trouble accepting it." After clearing his throat in discomfort, Biscane added, "She must have followed me into the house, perhaps with the intent of cornering me after my meeting with you. When she heard me declare that Jory is my mate, she said" — Biscane scowled as he thought over her words — "some confusing and troubling things."

"Lebone told me of her words after he had Pauline escort her back to the bunkhouse. That's why it took us so long to get over here," Bodb revealed with a nod. "I'd like permission for Attain and Ssimeas to round the hay." With a small smile curving his human lips, he turned his focus to Jory. "There is much to explain, but I see you don't seem to be freaking out. I must admit to being impressed."

Jory had been sweeping his gaze between them as they'd talked. His eyes had narrowed, and there was a contemplative expression on his face. Meeting Bodb's gaze squarely, he stated, "I have a lot of questions, but first" —he arched one brow as he smirked at Biscane—"the LeeAnn I met at the barbeque . . . the wrangler. She's one of your exes?"

"No," Biscane immediately replied. "I don't have exes. I've never been in a relationship."

"Then?" Jory pressed, drawing out the word.

Sighing deeply, Biscane admitted, "I had sex with her a few times several months ago. As far as I was concerned, it was a mutual desire to scratch an itch. Nothing more."

"But it seems she's not feeling the same?" Jory asked, cocking his head.

Biscane nodded. "Correct."

Jory nodded, too. "Okay. So what does this have to do with me? What's a mate again?"

Attain chuckled as he rounded the edge of the hay bales. There was a very slender gap that humans could use. Due to sporting wings, most gargoyles just went over the top.

"You really are starting backward, Biscane," Attain teased, stopping several feet away, keeping plenty of space between himself and the cot. He crossed his arms over his chest as he leaned against the wall of hay. "Just a quick question before we get to everything. Why aren't you freaking out, Jory? I know I did."

One side of Jory's mouth quirked up in a half-smile. "I spent a summer in New Orleans, so I already had a partial working knowledge that there were *other things*" —he lifted the hand that wasn't holding Biscane's and made air quotes— "out there." Scoffing, he continued, "Of course, that doesn't mean I don't have a shit-ton of questions. Biscane is tossing out a lot of terms I'm just not following."

"Not surprising," Ssimeas stated, dropping down from the hay to stand next to Attain. He immediately wrapped his arms around his human and pulled him back against him. "When a gargoyle or other paranormal meets his mate, the other half of his soul, he can get damn distracted and tongue-tied by the instant attraction." With a wink, he claimed, "It can make it hard to think straight."

Jory snorted softly. "Straight." He pointed at Attain. "So this mate thing can turn a straight man gay?"

Bodb shook his head. "No, it doesn't work quite like that." He pointed first at Attain and Ssimeas, then where Jory and Biscane still held hands. Jory looked down, his surprise clear, betraying that he hadn't even realized they were still doing that. "All Fate's pull does is ramp up the attraction that's already there."

"Hmmm, so you're saying that I would have found Biscane attractive even if there wasn't this mate thing between us?" Jory mused.

Pride flooded Biscane that his mate was catching on so swiftly, despite his half-assed non-explanations.

"Right," Bodb agreed.

Jory's eyes widened. "And that's why LeeAnn would be pissed," he muttered, putting everything together. He met Biscane's gaze squarely. "You had a fling. She thought it was more serious, and now that you're trying to move on, she's upset."

Biscane grimaced as he nodded once more.

Sighing, Jory rubbed the back of his neck. "I don't mean any offense, because they're right, I do find myself attracted to you, but how could we possibly have a relationship?" He furrowed his brows as he waved a hand between them. "I'm a human, and you're a gargoyle. Don't your kind turn to stone statues during the day?"

"Ah, so you have some knowledge of our kind." Biscane couldn't have been more pleased.

To Biscane's surprise, Jory snickered softly before saying, "Uh, I watched that *Gargoyles* cartoon when I was a kid, so—" He shrugged.

Attain grinned widely. "Hey! I loved that cartoon. I was so bummed when it got canceled."

"Me, too," Jory replied with a laugh. "Goliath was *hawt!*"

Biscane barely managed to keep in his growl upon hearing Jory compliment another, even a cartoon gargoyle.

Laughing, Attain replied, "I was always drooling over the detective chick. What was her name?"

Jory shook his head, still grinning. "Sorry. Don't remember."

"Do you have any idea what they're talking about?" Bodb cut in, sounding just as confused as Biscane felt.

"Nope," Ssimeas admitted.

Attain grinned broadly as he patted Ssimeas's hand where it rested on his stomach. "It sounds like we're going to be binge-watching *Gargoyles*," he declared. "I bet we can find it on some streaming channel somewhere."

"I'd like to see that, if you find it," Jory claimed. Then his cheeks took on a slightly pinkish hue, and embarrassment colored his scent. "Uh, if that's okay. Didn't mean to invite myself."

"It's fine," Bodb stated. "You're Biscane's mate, after all. I'm sure we'll be seeing a lot of you."

"Which brings us back to the question of having a relationship with a gargoyle." Jory glanced around the group, and his eyes narrowed. "Which you all don't seem to see a problem with."

"We don't," Bodb agreed. With an understanding smile, he revealed, "Because Ssimeas and I are also gargoyles."

"Uh, what?" Jory glanced from Biscane, to the other men, and back again, as if seeking reassurance from him. "How is that possible?"

Biscane flooded with pride that, even subconsciously, his mate looked to him. "Yes, a gargoyle does turn to stone during the day . . . until they find and bond with their mate," he explained, rubbing his thumb over Jory's wrist soothingly. "Once their bond is complete, then a gargoyle goes through a process called molt, where we gain a human form. Then we're able to stay awake during the day."

"Gain a human form," Jory repeated in a whisper. "Really?"

"Really," Attain confirmed. He eased forward a step and half-turned to face Ssimeas. "Will you show him, please?"

After Ssimeas looked at Bodb and received a nod of consent, he pulled his shirt over his head. Then he loosened the belt he wore a couple of holes before popping the top button. After that, he smiled at Jory.

"I'm going to show you my true form," Ssimeas warned. "I don't know if Biscane told you, but no paranormal here would ever harm you." Then he frowned as he muttered, "And if a human does, they're off the ranch."

"I'll second that," Bodb added gruffly.

Biscane scowled at the thought of anyone hurting Jory, LeeAnn in particular.

If my indiscretion somehow causes Jory any pain, I'll handle her the paranormal way.

Attacking a fated mate was against every code a paranormal lived by—well, most of them. There were rogues and traitors in every society. Still, those were getting fewer and farther between as all paranormal societies were coming together. The advancing technology made it more and more difficult for paranormals to live and hide in plain sight, so their leadership had begun communicating so they could work together. There were too many human anti-paranormal groups out there to stay separate.

In fact, the meeting Biscane was supposed to have attended with Elder Bodb and the other guards and enforcers was to be about security for an upcoming visit of a couple more gargoyle elders as well as two vampire council members. The ranch was going to have to be locked down tight to keep everyone safe.

Jory's gasp drew Biscane's attention to Ssimeas. The male was big in human form, standing six-foot-six and looking like a big, black football lineman. When he took on his true form, his skin adjusted to a dark-blue swarthy hide and his black hair disappeared, transitioning into large black horns on his head. He also gained several inches in height.

"Well, damn," Jory mumbled, staring at Ssimeas with wide eyes. "Th-That's . . . incredible."

"Pretty sweet, huh?" Attain said with a wide grin. Turning, he rubbed his palm over Ssimeas's naked chest. "Got my own gargoyle." Then Attain pointed at them. "And so do you. Accept it, and get the best damn sex of your life for as long as you both shall live." Then he scoffed. "Which will be for a really long time."

"What does that mean?" Jory quickly asked. "How long?"

"There's so much to explain," Bodb commented from where he still rested on the hay bales. He'd moved to sit cross-legged at some point with his palms resting on his knees. "Someone should make a slide presentation with all the bullet points we need to hit."

Scoffing, Attain shook his head. "Can you imagine if *that* fell into the wrong hands?"

Bodb nodded. "Good point." Raising one hand, he lifted one finger. "So, point one. Paranormals live a lot longer than humans but reproduce fewer offspring. Shifters, vampires, and those who wield magick normally live in the five-century range. Gargoyles live longer. Upward of a couple of millennia."

Jory's lips parted. "A couple of millennia?" he parroted. "As in . . . two *thousand* years?"

"Right." Ssimeas took up the explanation, holding up two fingers. "Because we're so long-lived, Fate gives us a soul mate, someone we can bond with who is our perfect complement. Once bonded, if the mate is a human, their life will extend to match the paranormal's." Ssimeas's expression turned serious as he added, "Now just because a paranormal's instinct is to please their other half doesn't mean it won't take work. Any relationship will always require work."

Attain nodded sagely. "Open communication and the willingness to compromise."

Jory also nodded. "That's understandable."

With how soft Jory's voice came out, Biscane got the impression that his mate was beginning to get overwhelmed. He rubbed his hand up and down his human's back, hoping to soothe. Still, he needed to explain a bit more before he could give Jory a chance to process.

"Point three," Biscane began softly, drawing Jory's focus. "Because we only get one mate, we are extremely possessive. While we strive to make our mate happy, to fulfill their needs, we also need our mate to be safe." Grimacing, he admitted, "That's why when LeeAnn claimed you weren't my mate, denying my bond with you, my need to get you away from her became damn near overwhelming. My instincts screamed at me to take you somewhere safe . . . especially since you aren't bonded with me yet, and your systems haven't become enhanced."

Narrowing his eyes, Jory nodded slowly. He licked his lips once, and Biscane wanted so badly to trace his own tongue along that line. Resisting, he waited. The others remained silent, too, obviously catching on to the fact that Jory needed a moment.

Blowing out a breath, Jory admitted, "There's so much more to the world than I thought." Before anyone could comment, he held up his free hand, asking for silence.

Biscane loved that throughout everything, Jory continued to hold his hand. It meant, on some level, he was open to his touch. His mate might have been reeling from information overload, but he wasn't afraid or averse to being with a gargoyle . . . or even a male, it seemed.

I wonder if he considers himself bisexual even though he's admitted to never being with a man before.

The idea of Jory admiring another — something in real life and not a cartoon — caused an irrational surge of jealousy, which Biscane swiftly squelched.

Stop being ridiculous.

"I have a couple of questions. Then I think I need time to process all this." Jory focused on Biscane. "Is that allowed? I don't want you to think I'm rejecting everything out of hand, but . . . well . . . I do my best thinking in my sauna at home."

"You have a sauna?"

The image of a hot, naked, and sweaty Jory reclining on a wooden bench in a steam-filled room popped into his mind. It had a predictable reaction on his body. His cock, which had softened during the serious conversation, surged back to full mast and even twitched behind his loincloth.

Jory glanced down, then snapped his gaze back to Biscane. "You like that idea," he whispered, clearly shocked.

Biscane chuckled huskily, seeing no point in hiding his need for his mate from Jory. "Anything involving you, naked or otherwise, will arouse me, Jory. You're my mate."

"Okay," Jory replied. "So, first question. Uh . . ."

Then Jory paused, frowning at the sheet covering them. He reached out, his hand hovering over Biscane's wing, as if he wanted to pet it again — perhaps as an absent gesture. Just before contact, Jory stopped himself.

While Biscane would have loved to feel Jory's hands on him, he knew it wasn't time for wing-play. He hoped they could do it again soon, though. Biscane had damn near come in his loincloth the first time Jory had stroked his wing.

Lifting his gaze and sweeping it around the group, Jory stated, "I get that this is important and a secret." He focused on Biscane. "I guess I don't even have questions, either. I don't even know where to begin, other than . . . I'm attracted to you. I can admit that to myself. I haven't thought about building a relationship with anyone in . . . a very long time." Smirking, Jory added, "A long time in human terms."

That earned a chuckle from the other men, while Biscane just smiled encouragingly at Jory. His heart hammered in his chest as he waited for whatever point his human was trying to make. He prayed to whatever god cared to listen that Jory wasn't about to reject him, no matter what his human had said earlier.

"Again, I'm not rejecting you or this or anything," Jory claimed as if he knew exactly what Biscane had been thinking, and he waved his hand in an absent manner. "I just need time to process." Offering a hint of a smile, Jory asked, "Maybe you could join me for dinner soon, and we can get to know each other?"

Biscane nodded once, happy to take anything Jory was willing to give him. "I'd like that." He reached over and grabbed his phone from the nearby nightstand where he'd placed it upon getting comfortable with his mate. "May I have your phone number?"

Jory nodded. "Yes, you may."

CHAPTER FIVE

Staring at the computer screen, Jory struggled to focus. The dream he'd woken from that morning still played through his mind hours later. For the first time in over twenty-five years, he'd woken hard as nails and ready to shoot. If he'd remained asleep for only a few minutes more, it would have ended up a wet dream.

In half a dozen strokes, Jory had been groaning with pleasure as his orgasm had swamped his system. He'd floated in bliss as he'd recalled how it'd felt to be touched and rubbed by Biscane's calloused hands. Of course, he knew it was just his brain's interpretation of how it could be from the feel of holding the gargoyle's hand.

Still, it had been fantastic.

Would it be like that in real life? It would be so easy to find out.

Jory had thought Biscane would call him sometime on Sunday . . . until he remembered that when the sun was in the sky, the male was a stone statue. It had been less than ten minutes after sunset when he'd received a text from Biscane. It had been simple, but it had still caused Jory's heart to race in his chest and his palms to sweat.

Thinking of you and wishing you were here. Can we have that dinner you mentioned Monday night?

Unable to wait, Jory had immediately replied. *Yes. Should I come to the ranch?*

Biscane had instantly responded — *What's your address?*

Without any hesitation, Jory had given Biscane the information.

The gargoyle's text had been swift to come. *I'll bring dinner. Do you have a favorite restaurant I can pick it up from?*

While Jory wasn't certain how a gargoyle could pick up take-out, he knew he couldn't ask that in writing. If anyone ever saw his phone, there was no way he wanted evidence of the paranormal on it. Not only could it be used against him in court, if the wrong person spotted it, but it could also be dangerous.

Jory wasn't so naive as to think everyone would be so accepting of things not human. With the number of hate groups that discriminated within their own race, he would bet his bottom dollar that there were already those who knew and hunted paranormals. Hell, if a poacher was willing to kill a rhinoceros simply for its horn, then imagine the money someone could make for a gargoyle horn.

Damn, not something so nice to think about.

The ring of Jory's phone nearly made him jump in his seat. He shook his head at himself as he reached for the handset. Checking the display, he saw that it was Jane Wandor, his secretary.

"Yes, Jane?" Jory said in lieu of a greeting.

"Hello, Mister Dartmore," Jane replied, telling Jory that there was someone in the outer office waiting to see him. "There's a Misses LeeAnn Tillerman here to see you." After a second, Jane added, "She says she's here to meet you for lunch, but I don't have anything on my schedule."

Jory narrowed his eyes as he rose from his seat. His suspicion caused his gut to tighten. While he hadn't heard LeeAnn's last name Saturday evening, he couldn't think of any other LeeAnns that he knew. If it was her, then her showing up was damn suspicious.

"There's nothing on the schedule because I didn't have lunch plans with anyone," he told his secretary. "Can you call Brakeman, please?"

"Of course, sir," Jane replied before hanging up.

Orem Brakeman was their head of security. If the coming scene played out the way Jory suspected, he wanted the level-headed, ex-military man's advice . . . and his support. That meant coming clean about planning to date a man.

Huh. When did I decide that?

Right. When I woke up this morning and had to rub one out before getting out of bed . . . then had to do it again in the shower.

Jory couldn't remember the last time he'd gotten a boner so swiftly, but if a heightened sexual drive was just one side effect of having a gargoyle lover, he wasn't going to be upset by it. He intended to call Attain as soon as he arrived home. After decompressing all day Sunday, add in the innocent texts that made his heart race, along with the anticipation filling him at seeing Biscane later that evening, he finally had a few questions.

Like, is this just a honeymoon phase until they bonded? Also, how did one bond with a gargoyle?

Pushing those thoughts aside, Jory focused on the matter at hand. He buttoned his suit jacket as he thought about what he could be facing. Jory had never been in a relationship, so he'd never had to face a spurned ex before. Deciding to play it as if she were the spouse of a client, Jory headed out of his office.

Keep it professional and have witnesses.

When Jory opened his office door, he was pleased to see that his moment of stalling had given Jane enough time to get Orem there. The man was seated in another waiting room chair and pretended to read a magazine. His nice polo shirt, sports coat, and slacks allowed him to blend, as if he were another waiting client.

Jory immediately spotted LeeAnn, who was rising from her own seat. In a light-tan skirt-suit outfit, he almost didn't recognize her. She had her thick blonde hair partly pulled away from her face, revealing her pretty features. The rest cascaded over her shoulders, disappearing behind her.

With a smile on her pale-red lips, Jory had to admit that she looked the part of a date to a powerful lawyer. She moved toward him confidently, holding out one hand as if she expected him to take it. In her other hand, she held a Vendetti's *to go* bag.

In truth, the aroma of the Italian food caused his mouth to water. For just an instant, he thought about accepting the meal just so he could enjoy the food. Then he spotted the cold glimmer in her blue eyes, and it acted just as good as a bucket of cold water on his head.

Right. So not happening.

Lifting a hand, Jory took LeeAnn's outstretched one. Even though she held it as if she expected him to kiss it, he didn't. He gave her a quick, perfunctory shake before releasing her.

"LeeAnn," Jory greeted with a dip of his head. "I'm surprised to see you here." Even though he knew it wasn't the case, he asked, "Are you here making an appointment to see someone in a legal capacity?"

LeeAnn tittered as she smiled brightly at him. "Of course not, silly." She held up the bag as if Jory hadn't noticed it. "I brought us lunch, sweetie."

Jory arched one brow. "Sweetie?" Shaking his head, he lifted his hands as if to ward her away. "I'm sorry, Miss Tillerman. There seems to be some kind of confusion. I'm not available for lunch today, and to be honest, I don't feel that it would be appropriate for us to share a meal without Biscane."

Tipping her head to the side, LeeAnn told him, "I'm certain Biscane wouldn't mind. We're all friends, after all."

"I'd call us acquaintances, LeeAnn," Jory countered. "After all, I've only met you once, in passing, at a mutual friend's barbeque." Moving closer to Jane's desk, he smiled at his secretary. "Is that flashing light my conference call?"

While Jory had no idea who was holding on line five, he knew it wasn't his conference call. He didn't have a conference call scheduled. Jory also knew that Jane would know that. They'd used the ruse to get rid of unwanted guests on more than one occasion.

The corners of Jane's lips quirked up just a smidge into a placid smile. "Not yet. I expect them in eight minutes."

Jory nodded. "Fantastic. Just enough time to use the men's room and get a cup of coffee." Then he turned, intending to return to his office to do just that.

"Wait a second, Jory," LeeAnn cried, grabbing his jacket sleeve. "I came all this way. You can't dismiss me like that. It's rude."

Jory paused and turned, tugging his sleeve free of her grip. "I'm sorry, LeeAnn. You've come to my place of work unannounced." Keeping his expression bland, he gave her the opening he hoped she would take, saying, "I don't really understand why you decided to show up today."

LeeAnn took the bait.

"I came to warn you that Biscane is a player," LeeAnn cried, grabbing his wrist in a tight grip. "He'll toss you away just as he did me." Stepping close, she hissed, "He claimed *I* was his mate just like he's doing to you. Once he gets what he wants, he'll toss you aside."

"Please remove your hand from Mister Dartmore," Orem ordered, having risen from his seat and moved next to them during her tirade. "Or I will remove it for you."

Snapping her attention to Orem, LeeAnn scowled at him. "This isn't any of your business."

"I'm security here, ma'am," Orem told her, moving his sports coat to the side to reveal the security tag attached to his belt. "When it comes to altercations, everything is my business."

LeeAnn unwound her fingers, causing a dull thud of pain to seep up Jory's arm, attesting to just how tight her grip had been.

Jory barely resisted the urge to rub at it. Instead, he kept his gaze neutral as he stated, "Thank you for the warning, LeeAnn. Perhaps I'll see you at the ranch sometime." With that dismissal, he turned and began heading back into his office.

"You'll be sorry," LeeAnn stated from behind him, but Jory ignored her.

Orem didn't. "Is that a threat, ma'am?"

"No," LeeAnn replied indignantly. "A warning. Biscane is only going to hurt him, just like he hurt me."

As Jory turned to close his door, he saw LeeAnn thrust the bag at Orem. "Here. Give him this. It may as well not go to waste." Then she pivoted and stalked to the door leading to the hall and the elevators.

Orem followed as far as the door, obviously watching to make certain she left.

Jory used the small ensuite bathroom attached to his office. Returning to his office proper, he moved to a side bar. He was very tempted to pour himself a couple fingers of whiskey, but he resisted.

It was just past noon, and he had a meeting with a client that afternoon. It wouldn't do to go with liquor on his breath. With a sigh, he opted for a decaf coffee pod and slipped it into the machine.

As his cup of joe poured, Jory watched his office door open. Orem appeared as well as Jane. His secretary was carrying the Vendetti's bag, and she placed it on the coffee table.

"She sounded a little vindictive," Orem stated without preamble, crossing his arms over his chest. "Like you stole her boyfriend or something." His eyes narrowed just a little as he tipped his chin toward the bag. "As much as I love Vendetti's, I'm not certain I'd trust anything from her."

Jory sighed deeply as he picked up his finished mug. "Sadly, I'm afraid you're right." Then he moved to a chair, but instead of sitting in it, he rested his hip against the backrest.

"Too bad, because I am hungry."

Jane moved to the coffee station. "You want anything, Orem?"

"Coffee would be great," the security chief replied. "Thanks, Jane."

Wincing, Jory muttered, "Sorry. Being a bad host."

Orem scoffed. "Seems you have something else on your mind." A hint of a smile curved the left corner of the big man. "You gonna tell us what that is?"

"You have seemed a bit distracted this morning," Jane pointed out as she started the coffee machine. "Is it that Biscane person that LeeAnn mentioned?"

Jory nodded. "It is." These were the two people whose support he would need the most.

And Reginald, but I'll talk to him soon.

"I met Biscane Saturday night," Jory told them. "He sort of . . . swept me off my feet." *Literally, not that I can tell them that.* "Can't say I've ever been so captivated so swiftly by anyone, man or woman."

"And Biscane dated LeeAnn at some point, and she's not happy he's moving on."

While Orem didn't make it a question, Jory nodded anyway.

"How'd she find out about your interest so fast?" Jane asked curiously, handing over a cup of coffee to Orem while keeping one for herself. "I mean, I don't know about you guys, but when I start dating someone, I don't make it a habit to immediately tell my exes." Jane's dark brows furrowed as she mused, "Unless Biscane was still dating LeeAnn and he had to break up with her before taking you on a date?"

Discomfort flooded Jory. He'd never discussed his personal life at work before. Tapping his fingers on the back of the chair he leaned against, he tried to decide the best way to answer.

Finally, Jory went with the truth. "Biscane admits to being

something of a player in the past," he began slowly. "LeeAnn wasn't someone he dated. She was someone he slept with occasionally, although he stopped several months ago, and she's been trying to get him to resume their liaisons ever since."

"He's open about his past," Orem commented before taking a sip of his coffee. "That's a good thing. Means he's serious."

"Well, when one of your hook-ups lives and works at the same ranch as you do, you kind of have to be," Jory told them.

Orem grunted, then swallowed hard. He wiped the corner of his lip as he sucked in a harsh breath. His wide brown eyes betrayed the deeply tanned-skinned man's surprise.

Jane shook her head and pursed her lips. "It's never a good idea to mix work and pleasure." She winked at Orem. "Sorry, big guy. I'll never go on a date with you."

Orem regained his composure and let out a soft chuckle. "I'll try to contain the depth of my disappointment, beautiful."

Jory snorted quietly, appreciating his co-workers' attempts at levity. He knew neither one of them were actually interested in each other. They enjoyed teasing though, and the banter helped relieve tension in a high-stress environment.

"You'll need to tell Biscane that LeeAnn stopped by," Jane told him with a firm nod.

"Want me to have the food checked for anything . . . that could cause problems for you?" Orem offered, pointing at the paper sack.

His gut clenching, and not from hunger, Jory asked, "You think she would try to poison me or something?"

Shrugging one big shoulder, Orem grabbed the bag. "Better safe than sorry, so you know what you're dealing with . . . or not dealing with." Then he grinned broadly and held up the bag. "And if it's clean, I'll have something tasty to eat."

Laughing, his tension draining, Jory waved Orem away. "Got it. Enjoy."

"And *I'll* order you a real lunch," Jane told him, moving toward the door. "Maybe some fried, fatty comfort food," she teased, knowing he rarely ate that.

Right then, however, it sounded damn good, so Jory nodded and smiled.

"Fried chicken and biscuits," Jane announced as she swept out of the room.

Jory's stomach growled just at the idea, since he knew where she would be ordering that from.

Yum!

Orem followed. "And I'll add LeeAnn to the list of people banned from our offices."

"Thanks. To you both," Jory called, watching them disappear.

Then Jory returned to work, although he found it extremely difficult to focus.

CHAPTER SIX

As soon as roost released its bonds, Biscane jumped to his feet. He immediately scowled. "LeeAnn, what are you doing here?"

LeeAnn smiled brightly at him and held out a mug. "I brought you some coffee. With everything going on, I figured you'd be pressed for time."

"Thank you," Biscane stated, wariness surging through him as he reached out and took the mug. As he brought the cup to his lips, he spotted the expectant gleam in LeeAnn's eyes. Hesitating with the drink a couple of inches from his lips, he asked, "Is there something else?"

"Did I get enough sugar in it?"

Everyone knew that Biscane wasn't a real big fan of coffee. He doctored it up with excessive amounts of cream and sugar to hide the flavor. Even the high-end stuff that Bodb favored when he wasn't drinking tea was too rich for Biscane's preferences.

It was sort of a running joke at the ranch because they went through a lot of sugar because of him.

Biscane lifted the mug the rest of the way to his lips and took a tiny, tentative sip. The sweetness of sugar and the flavor of a pumpkin spice creamer flowed across his tongue, hiding the taste of the coffee. Taking a larger swallow, he smiled his thanks.

Then Biscane turned and picked up his phone. As he swallowed another mouthful, he felt the hot liquid warm his stomach. He spotted a text from Jory, sent just a few minutes before, wishing him a good morning, and his blood heated as he thought of his mate waiting for him to bring dinner, firming up his morning wood.

"Do you need help with that?" LeeAnn asked sultrily as she boldly skimmed a hand along his side, reaching around to his front.

Jumping sideways as if burned, Biscane jerked from her touch. His breathing sped up as his hide tingled where she'd been stroking him. Even his cock throbbed, shocking the shit out of him.

"What the hell?" Biscane muttered, confusion thrumming through him. As a paranormal, he shouldn't be aroused by anyone other than his mate now that he'd met him. What the hell was going on? Why was his body responding to LeeAnn's touch?

Taking advantage of his confusion, LeeAnn stepped forward and placed her palms on his chest. "Just relax, handsome," she crooned, rubbing over his pectorals. "Let's have some fun before you start the day."

Biscane's nipples beaded, and a shudder worked through his body. He burned with arousal, his shaft aching insistently. His unexpected need clouded his mind, making it difficult to think.

"N-No, I d-don't—" he began to stutter, struggling to remember why sinking his aching cock into what he knew was a warm, wet, and inviting pussy was a bad idea.

"Of course you want to," LeeAnn countered huskily. "You love the way my wet sheath milks your hard cock."

LeeAnn's hands lowering to his hips caused his erection to twitch, eager for touch, for the chance to do just that. He could slide into her depths, plunder her body, and satisfy his base instinct. The need to rut muddled his thoughts, and he gripped her hips as he turned his gaze to the cot he'd just risen from.

Just as Biscane took a step forward, intending to guide Lee-Ann onto it, he heard Stanley holler, "Biscane! You still up here?" Then he appeared around the corner. Surprise colored the Native American's features as he glanced between them and asked, "Biscane, what's going on?"

Biscane swallowed hard, trying to get moisture into his mouth and for his brain to unscramble for a few seconds.

"We'll be down in a few minutes, Stanley," LeeAnn told him. "You know his shift doesn't officially start for an hour after waking from roost, and I'm already off work for the day."

Even Biscane's confused mind heard the silent *get lost* in her tone. He opened his mouth to second LeeAnn's claim, but Stanley asked, "What about Jory, Biscane? I thought he was your mate."

"Jory," Biscane whispered, his thoughts clearing a little. Frowning, he admitted, "He is."

"Then what the hell are you doing?" Stanley demanded again.

"I-I . . ." *What the hell* am *I doing?* "I don't know."

Stanley lifted his phone to his ear and stated, "Emergency in the loft. I need an assist asap."

"Obviously Biscane was mistaken about that human," Lee-Ann countered, rubbing over his chest once more. "After all, if that were the case" — she sounded smug as hell — "he wouldn't be wanting me."

That was true, right?

Except, Biscane knew he wasn't wrong about Jory. Every instinct in him had screamed to care for, pleasure, and protect the human. He'd wanted to make him his, claim and bite him, and to have Jory do that to him in return.

Then why do LeeAnn's touches feel so amazing?

Biscane sighed as he pressed into her hands, enjoying the zings of pleasure they caused. His balls rolled in his sack, and he began to reach for the stays of his loincloth. He knew if he didn't get himself buried balls deep in LeeAnn's pussy damn soon, he'd spill in the fabric.

"LeeAnn, step away from Biscane," a deep angry voice roared. "Now!"

With a huff, LeeAnn obeyed, taking a step back and lowering her hands. "What a bunch of cock-blockers," she grumbled, turning away from Biscane. "We're two consenting adults. I don't see the issue."

"Get out of here, LeeAnn."

Without LeeAnn touching him, Biscane finally recognized Elder Bodb's voice. He blinked once, twice, trying to focus. Glancing around, he realized that not only had Bodb arrived, but so had Lebone, Ssimeas, and Gladstone — one of Bodb's brothers — and Spieron — one of the ranch's resident vampires.

Even with the audience, Biscane still found his gaze straying to LeeAnn's backside as she swept around Stanley and disappeared from view. The second she was no longer in sight, he felt as if a fog had lifted from his mind. He stumbled back a few steps, hitting the hay behind him, as he realized what he'd been about to do.

"Holy shit," Biscane whispered roughly. He scrubbed over his chest, feeling beyond dirty. "What the hell happened?"

"Good question," Bodb said with a growl still in his voice. "If Stanley hadn't arrived, I'm certain you would have fucked her . . . without protection."

While gargoyles could only impregnate fated male mates, without precautions, they were like any other male. They could get any female pregnant. Male mates always produced an egg which would hatch into a gargoyle. With females, it was a fifty-fifty shot, just like any other pregnancy.

Biscane had never been careless enough to screw a woman without precautions. As much as he wanted a child, he only wanted one with his mate. He never wanted to be tied to anyone who wasn't that Fate-given special someone.

Except, Biscane knew Bodb was right. He'd had only one thing on his mind — getting inside LeeAnn. What Biscane didn't understand was why.

"I thought once we met our mate, only they could arouse us," Biscane murmured, rubbing the back of his neck and feeling dirtier than he'd ever felt in his life. "How could she turn me on so much and so fast that I'd forget . . . everything?"

Including my mate.

When Biscane's gut clenched, he fought the urge to hurl, disgust permeating every inch of him.

"While that's true, it's only *after* you bond," Bodb corrected. "Before that, you'll still be able to be turned on by others, but I've never heard of any paranormal acting like you just did."

"Shit," Biscane said on a groan. "I need a shower." A pang of regret stabbed his heart, but at least it killed his boner. "And pray to the gods that my mate will forgive me."

"This really doesn't make sense," Stanley pointed out, shaking his head. "You've been avoiding LeeAnn for months, and she's been trying to change your mind. And I heard what she said when you found Jory."

"Right," Lebone agreed. "After everything I did, she'd said."

"What'd she do?" Ssimeas asked curiously. "Did anyone ever find out?"

"She's one of the one percent of humans a vampire can't affect, so I can't get into her mind to find out," Spieron told them. His gaze narrowed, and his tone turned malicious. "Unless you give me leave to use alternate means of persuasion."

Bodb groaned softly. "I hate to go that route with people we're supposed to trust."

After a deep inhale, Lebone pointed at the cup. "Where'd

you get the coffee? I know you haven't been to the kitchen, yet."

"LeeAnn brought it," Biscane admitted.

"And you drank it?"

Biscane heard Stanley's incredulity, reminding him of his own distrust. "I didn't taste anything in it."

"Give it here," Ssimeas ordered, beckoning with his fingers.

Stanley crossed the room and grabbed it before Biscane could. He handed it to the other gargoyle, who sniffed at it.

"You think it's laced with something?" Biscane asked. As much as that would suck, it gave him hope that he hadn't been acting of his own accord. "Can a gargoyle be drugged?"

"You know I take a daily potion to render me infertile," Ssimeas reminded him. "There *are* things that can affect us."

The gargoyle was one of the few of their population that was immune to the effects of cinnamon—normally a natural contraceptive. His mate, Attain, was allergic to the spice. That meant the pair had found an alternate method of birth control . . . a potion from their ranch's resident witch—Maggie.

Biscane would never suspect Maggie of purposefully tampering with anyone's drinks, but that didn't mean there weren't witches out there who would . . . for a price. Not everyone was as honorable as Maggie. Plus, her familiar, Sandra—the equivalent of a soul mate to a witch—was best friends and formerly the spouse of Bodb's mate, Nicholas.

Most everyone on the ranch was close.

"Oh, damn," Lebone grumbled, wrinkling his nose. "There's definitely something in that."

"Oh?" Spieron took the mug and sipped it. He scowled. "Huh. You're right. I taste something I can't identify."

"How come I didn't notice it?" Biscane asked, confused even as a bit of relief filled him, too.

Lebone smirked at Biscane. "Because when it comes to coffee, you try *not* to taste it."

Biscane sighed and nodded. "Yeah." Glancing around the group, he asked, "So, how do we find out what she put in it and make her leave me alone?"

If Biscane never saw LeeAnn again, it would be too soon. *And never will I take any food and drink from her ever again.*

"I'll take it to Maggie and see if she can identify it," Ssimeas told them, taking the cup and turning away.

"And I give you permission to use more . . . *persuasive* tactics on LeeAnn," Bodb stated with a touch of sad frustration in his tone. "We can't have her messing with mate-bonds, and we need to know what other kind of shit she might be willing to pull."

Biscane bent his knees and leaped, landing on the top of the hay. "I'm going to head to the shower," he told everyone. Pausing, he turned his head and peered at Stanley. "Thank you. I am truly in your debt."

Stanley smiled faintly at him while shaking his head. "Don't thank me. I should have checked into LeeAnn's activities earlier. I'm the foreman, and I'm supposed to be in charge of making certain the ranch runs smoothly." Grimacing, he added, "That includes making certain that interpersonal relationships don't cause trouble."

"We all ignored the way LeeAnn has been chasing after Biscane," Bodb pointed out. "And I think we may need to implement your policy of never sleeping with co-workers."

It was well known by everyone that Stanley never slept with anyone employed at the ranch. Biscane had tried to get the handsome Native American into bed a time or two himself. The human had always kindly rebuffed him.

Now Biscane was very glad that he had.

"Unless they turn out to be mates, of course," Gladstone cut in.

"Right," Bodb agreed.

Slapping Biscane on the shoulder, Lebone encouraged, "Go get cleaned up. Lludd is on his way with your order from Chen's." With a reassuring smile, he added, "And Pauline has a wonderful sake set aside that will go fantastic with the sushi Jory told you he enjoyed."

Biscane nodded. "Thank you."

Then Biscane jumped down from the other side of the hay and started toward the loft door. Just as he reached it, Ssimeas returned, the mug still in hand.

"Bad news," Ssimeas called, peering beyond Biscane at their elder. "LeeAnn took off in her private vehicle. I checked her room, and it's empty of almost everything personal as well as half the clothes."

Growling low in his throat, Bodb rumbled, "She's running."

Smirking, Spieron waggled his eyebrows. "I guess she didn't know that Darian's beloved is a damn paranoid ex-military man," he stated. "He had trackers put in every vehicle." Grimacing, Spieron met Bodb's gaze. "Sorry, Elder. Even yours."

Darian was the second vampire living at the ranch. He'd once been part of the same coven as Spieron, but when he'd found his beloved in the human, Claude, he'd been forced to leave. Unfortunately, Claude had run afoul of a demon and had his mind messed with, giving him the equivalent of PTSD.

If Claude had a flashback, he would start going after humans and trying to save paranormals. The coven had too many donors, and they hadn't been equipped to handle Claude's issues. With so many gargoyles and other paranormals around with only a few humans left there, they were able to easily handle the occasional incident.

"If I had a demon mess with my mind, I'd be paranoid, too," Bodb claimed, dismissing Claude's actions with a wave of his hand. "Besides, his need to protect Darian is a boon to us. Go drop the coffee off with Maggie and explain what's happening." Bodb focused on Spieron. "Find Darian and Claude and explain what's going on. I want to know where LeeAnn is headed before Biscane heads to his mate's."

Within seconds, everyone scurried to obey, murmuring *yes, elders.*

Biscane headed to the bunkhouse, where he took a long, scalding-hot shower and tried his best to squelch the guilt plaguing him.

CHAPTER SEVEN

Jory relaxed on his veranda, staring at the view. He'd lit the metal fire pit, and the heat helped fight the slight chill of the evening air. The glass of white wine he sipped did the same to his insides.

Peering into the distance, Jory could just make out the movement of people jogging on the path by the river. The lights of the park sparkled off the water. Coupled with the lights of the street far below him, he saw that when he looked up, he couldn't see the stars.

Lifting his wrist, he checked the time on his *Rolex*. The sun had set almost an hour and a half ago, and Biscane had told him he hoped to get to him within the hour. His stomach churned with discomfort as he thought of LeeAnn's words.

He told me I was his mate, too. He's just using you.

Jory really didn't want to believe the woman, but what did he really know about the gargoyle? Hell, what did he know about paranormals in general? Only what he'd been told by the people at Nicholas's ranch.

Except, Attain lived out there, too.

While Jory had never considered Attain a friend while working together, he thought they'd moved in that direction. Surely Attain would have told him if any of what the gargoyles had told him was a lie. The man was way too straight-laced to perpetuate a manipulation.

After taking a sip of his wine, Jory placed the glass on the nearby table. He held his hands out to the fire and tried to control his thoughts. Even though those guys were the first paranormals he'd ever met, he didn't think that changed his ability to accurately judge their character.

"Jory."

Hearing Biscane's deep voice behind him and to the right, Jory jolted in his seat. He turned and stared into the darkness. Due to looking into the fire and watching the flames, he had to squint to even make out a hint of an outline.

"Biscane?" Jory whispered.

Then he wanted to smack himself upside the head. Instead, he mentally rolled his eyes. Who else would show up at his place via a veranda that was seventeen stories up?

"Hi, Jory." Biscane moved into view, folding his billowing black wings over his shoulders, giving him the appearance of wearing a cloak. "I'm sorry I'm so much later than I'd hoped, my mate. Please forgive me."

Rising from his seat, Jory took in Biscane's pensive expression. "Is everything okay?" He had news of his own, but he didn't want to burden the gargoyle first thing.

Biscane shook his head. "Afraid not, and I wish to share it with you." Placing a soft-sided cooler bag on the metal and glass table, he admitted, "I want nothing but the truth between us, even when it's uncomfortable."

Jory took a chance, reaching out and touching Biscane's thick wrist. "I'd like that, too."

"Thank you." Biscane turned his hand and threaded their fingers together. Then he grabbed a chair, pulled it closer to Jory's, and settled on it. "Please, sit with me."

Easing back onto his seat, Jory picked up his wine glass. "Can I get you a drink before we start any heavy conversation?"

After releasing Jory's hand, Biscane opened the bag. "I have something that will go good with our meal." Softly, he added, "Assuming you still want to see me after my confession."

"Well, that doesn't sound ominous at all," Jory murmured as he watched Biscane open a side pocket and pull out a bottle. "We've both already admitted to never being in a relationship, so we're bound to screw up every now and then." As Jory read the label — a very nice sake that he was familiar with and enjoyed — he decided to just throw his fears out there. "Unless you were lying about the whole mate thing. Are you here just to scratch an itch?"

If that was all that was going on, Jory wanted to know upfront.

"No!" Biscane barked, appearing stricken. "I would *never* lie about such a thing. Never!" He set the glass tumblers he'd pulled from the bag on the table with a clatter, then grabbed one of Jory's hands between both of his own. "You are my mate, Jory Dartmore. The other half of my soul. My very reason for every breath I take and every beat of my heart. Please believe me."

Hearing the near begging quality of Biscane's tone, Jory couldn't help but believe him. "Okay." He smiled and squeezed the hand within his own. "So tell me what has you so upset."

It was obvious something had happened to create such disquiet within Biscane. Jory had a funny feeling that normally the male was cool and confident. He'd certainly acted that way a couple of nights before, and Jory guessed that was his natural personality.

Biscane bowed his head, staring at the faux-stone flooring. After nodding once, he lifted his head and met Jory's gaze. "LeeAnn slipped something in my coffee, and I almost slept with her," Biscane blurted. "If Stanley hadn't interrupted us because he suspected she was up to something, I would have."

"She slipped something in your coffee," Jory repeated slowly. "You took coffee from her? Why?"

He needed facts before he allowed his mind to jump to conclusions.

"Yes. In my morning coffee." Grimacing, Biscane explained, "I don't like coffee, so I hide the taste with a lot of cream and sugar. Everyone at the ranch knows this." With a huff, he grumbled, "I can't believe I didn't realize she was up to something when she brought it to me just as I woke from roost. She's never done that before, but I was so preoccupied with coming to see you that I wasn't thinking straight." Biscane furrowed his brow ridges as his focus slipped back to the ground. He blinked a few times as a pained expression came over his features. "Then after a few sips, I wasn't thinking at all. I didn't even feel in control. There was just this . . . burning *need*. This desire to fuck, to sink my hard cock into the closest willing body, which happened to be LeeAnn, and I—"

Having heard enough, Jory pressed his fingertips against the gargoyle's lips. The male immediately shut up and met his gaze. The anguish and guilt swimming within the depths of Biscane's sparkling black eyes nearly took his breath away.

"You were drugged, Biscane," Jory whispered softly. "You weren't in control. I understand."

Biscane's shoulders sagged a little. Then he straightened, pulling away and murmuring, "Thank you for understanding."

Jory shrugged. "Well, at least she's trying to sleep with you." Smirking, he admitted, "She's trying to kill me."

"What?" Biscane demanded loudly with a growl in his voice. His wings lifted from his shoulders, displaying his alarm even more than his tone as he demanded, "What's that mean?"

Reaching for his glass of wine, Jory took a sip before answering. "Well, LeeAnn showed up at the office today with lunch," he explained. "Since I'd only met her in passing at the barbeque, and after the things you talked about with your fellow, uh, friends, it seemed damn suspicious to me. I sent her away, but she left the food." Knowing he had to be just as honest as Biscane, Jory added, "After issuing a few veiled threats." When he spotted the gargoyle's flared nostrils and angry expression, he quickly told the male, "I've had her barred from the building."

Biscane nodded once as he took a couple of slow, deep breaths, obviously trying to settle down. His voice came out a bit gruff when he stated, "I'm so very glad you're okay." He swallowed so hard his Adam's apple bobbed before he asked, "How do you know she's trying to kill you?"

"Right. I didn't really explain that, did I?" Jory mused. He pointed at the bag. "How about dinner?"

After continuing to stare at him for a few heartbeats, Biscane began pulling out clear-plastic cartons full of sushi.

Jory hummed as his mouth watered. He didn't usually eat so late, so he was quite hungry. Of course, he wouldn't ever tell that to Biscane, since the male couldn't control his limitations.

Unless we bond.

Just that thought caused Jory's blood to heat and his ass to clench. It wasn't all trepidation, either . . . although some of it *definitely* was. He was old enough to have had a couple of prostate exams, and he certainly hadn't enjoyed them. Jory had no idea how shoving something as large as the average dick up his chute could be enjoyable, and Biscane was far larger than that, considering the bulge that he'd noticed Saturday evening.

"Something just upset you," Biscane commented, reaching over and gripping Jory's wrist. He gently massaged his pulse point with his thumb. Lowering his voice, he added, "I don't mean to upset you. I just need to know how to protect you."

Clearing his throat, Jory fought back the sensation of his cheeks heating. "Well, I think we can both agree never to eat or drink anything that LeeAnn gives us," he stated. "She sprinkled the salad with arsenic. Enough to make me damn sick if it didn't kill me outright." For a second, Jory thought about leaving it at that, but he decided to be honest, too. "And I tensed up because I thought about bonding. I talked to Attain about it this evening after work, and I . . . I must admit I'm a bit . . . concerned."

Biscane's thick lips parted for a second before a wide smile curved them. A hungry gleam entered his eyes — this one not for food. After clearing his throat, he grinned as he returned to opening the food.

As Biscane poured sake into the small tumblers that he'd brought, he murmured, "I want you to know, when the time comes, I'll make your body sing with pleasure." Biscane set the bottle down and turned his full attention on Jory. "I intend to make you orgasm multiple times, ending with so much bliss, your system will overload, and you'll pass out."

"Pass out from pleasure?" Jory thought this was a much better conversation than LeeAnn and her poisoning. "Never had that happen before." Chuckling, he admitted, "While forty-two might not be old for a gargoyle, it's past a human's sexual prime. Multiple orgasms may be too much to hope for."

Biscane growled softly, the sound husky with desire. "I know you don't mean that as a challenge, but I'm taking it as one." Then he winked. "So, let's forget the unpleasantness of the day, eat, and get to know each other."

"Sounds like a plan to me," Jory agreed, taking the chopsticks Biscane handed him. He opened them as he perused the offerings Biscane had spread over his outdoor table. "You bought all my favorites and then some," he acknowledged as he picked up a roll of spicy shrimp tempura. "No way can we eat all this stuff, and sushi leftovers don't keep long."

Biscane's deep chuckles rolled through the air. When Jory

arched one brow, the male told him, "One of the things you'll learn about paranormals is that we have much larger appetites than most humans." He swept his clawed finger in a circle, pointing at everything spread on the table. "There won't be much left. I assure you."

"Wow. Really?" Before Jory popped the sushi roll into his mouth, he asked, "How does Pauline keep up with all of you?"

Waggling his eyebrow ridges, Biscane revealed, "She's a red fox shifter, so she grew up with paranormal appetites." Then he grabbed a lobster roll between the claws of his thumb and forefinger before popping it into his mouth.

Jory coughed a little, doing everything possible to keep his mouth shut so he didn't spray half-chewed food across the table. Once he'd regained his breathing, he swallowed. He grabbed his wine glass, took a sip, and swallowed. Then he repeated.

After inhaling deeply and no longer needing to cough, Jory scowled at Biscane.

The huge gargoyle sported a sheepish expression and quickly swallowed his own bite of food. "I'm sorry," he told him. "I didn't mean to make you choke." Reaching over, he rubbed up and down Jory's back. "Are you okay?"

Jory scoffed softly. "Yeah, I'm okay." Shaking his head, he smirked at the troubled-looking Biscane. "Guess I need to get used to those types of comments."

"Yeah?" Biscane sounded questioning, hopeful.

Realizing what his comment could imply—that he intended to be around a while—Jory just nodded and shrugged. Then he winked and grabbed another roll with his chopsticks. He dipped it into a container of soy sauce Biscane had put out before popping it into his mouth.

"I like the sound of that," Biscane told him before picking up another roll, too.

After swallowing, Jory asked, "So, tell me about paranormals."

Over the next couple of hours, Biscane did just that. He shared many facts about the different species of paranormals — types, hierarchies, and abilities — and he answered Jory's every question. Never once did he appear annoyed or bored when Jory asked for clarification on things.

Jory found the information fascinating. He also enjoyed listening to the deep timbre of Biscane's voice. The male continued eating long after Jory had finished, but he didn't mind. Jory just sat back with his sake glass and enjoyed Biscane's company as they discussed the new world he found himself in.

Finally, Biscane began packing all the leftover rolls — which counted six pieces — into one container. "Would you like to take this to work tomorrow?"

Humming appreciatively, Jory nodded. "Sure. I'd like that." Then a yawn took him by surprise. His jaw popped a bit as he covered his mouth. Shaking his head once, he mumbled, "Sorry about that."

Biscane rested his hand over Jory's. "It's okay. I'm sure this is late for you." With a glance toward the moon, he added, "It's almost eleven-thirty."

"Damn, really?" Jory couldn't remember the last time he'd stayed up that late on a weekday. "Guess I better get to bed."

The thought of a bed coupled with Biscane touching him created a warm flush through his system. It could have been caused by a mix of the alcohol, too. He wouldn't call himself inebriated, but he'd definitely had a bit more than his standard couple of glasses of wine with a meal.

"Yes, Jory," Biscane rumbled. "Let's get you to bed."

Biscane was on his feet, sweeping Jory into his arms, before he could comment. Unable to help himself, as he found himself carried into his condo and through the space, he chuckled. Shaking his head, he relaxed.

Being the smaller in a pairing was a damn novel experience.

"I can walk, you know," Jory had to tease.

"I know, but I like this so much better."

Oddly enough, Jory didn't mind. Of course, he would never, ever admit that out loud . . . to anyone. Instead, he just pointed where he needed to go.

Biscane placed him on his feet in the middle of his bedroom. The gargoyle glanced toward his bed, then cleared his throat. "I'll, uh, leave you to get changed and, um, put the sushi in the fridge."

As Biscane rushed from the room, Jory wondered if he'd done something wrong. Except, then the man paused and half-turned to look at him. The longing in his gaze combined with the tell-tale bulge told Jory everything he needed to know.

He wants me.

Turning to the bathroom, Jory thought about that as he changed and cleaned up for the night.

While Jory knew he wasn't ready for full-on sex, his half-hard prick told him there were other things his body wouldn't mind enjoying.

Hope he comes back soon.

Unfortunately, as soon as Jory relaxed on his bed to wait, the crazy day caught up with him, and he slipped off to sleep.

CHAPTER EIGHT

Waking from roost in a bedroom at the main house, Biscane remained relaxed on the cushioned window seat for a few minutes. He thought about the prior evening and smiled. His mate had been so exhausted that he'd fallen asleep before Biscane had finished putting everything away.

That also means he's comfortable with me in his space.

Biscane was going to take that as a win. He was taking the fact that his mate wasn't upset about the almost-fucking-Lee-Ann thing as a win, too. While it was true that he'd been under the influence of something—extract of allecorde, a rare plant, according to Maggie—he should have had more self-control than that.

Never going to allow that to happen again.

Unfortunately, Maggie hadn't been able to tell them where LeeAnn had gotten it. She hadn't sensed anyone using magick in the area. Magick-users didn't sense spell-use quite the same way as how a vampire could tell when another in their area used their mind abilities.

Vampires experienced something that felt like ripples of a pond lapping in their mind, giving them direction and power.

Maggie explained that, unless they were mentally searching for a witch or warlock using their powers, they wouldn't notice it.

My mate looked so gorgeous sprawled on his bed.

When Biscane had returned from sorting everything on the veranda, he'd found Jory resting half propped up with pillows. He wore a pair of navy green sleep pants and a black tank top. One leg was cocked to the side, and the other was half under the covers.

It looked like he'd been trying to wait for Biscane, but his fatigue had gotten the better of him.

Biscane had stared at Jory for several long minutes, watching him sleep. He'd been tempted to slip into bed and wake him in the most pleasurable of ways. He'd also thought about just lying there and holding him for a while.

Finally, Biscane chose to ease Jory down the bed a little. He'd pulled the blanket over his body and tucked him in. After pressing a kiss to his forehead, taking a second to flick out his tongue and lick his mate's skin, he'd left him to sleep.

Once Biscane had confirmed the doors and windows were shut and locked, he exited via the veranda. He'd locked the door behind him, gathered his satchel, and made his way to the edge. After admiring the view for several minutes, Biscane realized he was just procrastinating in leaving his mate.

With a smile permanently etched across his features, he'd returned home.

A soft tapping pulled Biscane out of his thoughts. "Come," he urged, turning his head to peer toward the door, although he didn't bother rising.

Gladstone and Lludd walked into the room, both in their natural forms. They were followed by Lludd's mate, Sheriff Archer Montgomery. The human had jurisdiction over the county where most of the ranch was located, but not the city where Jory lived.

Swinging his legs off the side of the bench seat, Biscane straightened. "Hi, guys," he greeted, glancing between them, wondering at the need for human law enforcement. "What's up?"

"I tracked down LeeAnn," Archer stated without preamble. "She's dead."

"I, uh . . . what?" *Real eloquent, Biscane.*

"I told you he didn't do it," Lludd stated.

Archer smirked at Lludd. "And I told you I didn't think he did, but I had to see his face when he found out."

Frowning, Biscane demanded, "What the hell is going on?"

"Actually, we're not entirely sure," Gladstone admitted, shoving his hands into the front pockets of his jeans. "We followed Claude's directions to LeeAnn's car. She was parked at a trailhead north of here," he told him. Frowning, he continued, "She was in the driver's seat, and she had a bullet hole in her forehead."

Sighing, the sheriff picked up the explanation. "She looked surprised. Like she knew her attacker."

"And there wasn't any blood spatter on the seat of the car," Lludd cut in. "So she was obviously moved, but there were no drag marks."

Archer nodded. "Right. Which means her killer was strong enough to carry her and position her in her car." With a deep sigh, he added, "My people show several suspicious deposits in her checking account over the last few months as well as some odd online purchases."

"That's where the allecorde came from," Lludd revealed. "So that's a relief."

"Yeah, but how did she know what it was and how to use it?" Biscane decided he was more unsettled by the fact that a plant extract that could affect gargoyles in such a manner was being sold online to whoever wanted it. "Can we track the seller?"

"Claude is already working on that," Gladstone promised.

Relief filled Biscane.

While Claude had his problems, hacking was not one of them. Even though he'd been a sniper in the military—then in the private sector, which was where he'd tangled with the demon—the man had taken to cyber warfare with ease. A wolf shifter and his human mate had passed through their area not too long ago, and the human — Jared — had been more than happy to teach Claude everything he could . . . which was a lot.

"I didn't hear that," Archer muttered, glaring at Gladstone.

Gladstone shrugged and smirked.

Archer rolled his eyes, then turned back to face Biscane. "My guess is whatever was going on with LeeAnn isn't ending with her death, so watch yourself." After a heartbeat, he added, "And watch your mate. Congratulations, by the way."

Biscane couldn't help but smile. "Thank you, Sheriff. I'm overjoyed to have found Jory."

"Just remember, Jory Dartmore is pretty high-profile," Archer warned. "Even more high-profile than Attain or Nicholas. He's in the news every once in a while after fighting cases for socialites and rich people." Crossing his arms over his chest, he furrowed his brows. "Between this and that, you might want to consider the idea of more security."

"Already on the docket," Gladstone stated. "Although not because of Jory." Then he pointed at the sheriff. "But thank you for the warning." Gladstone turned his attention back to Biscane. "Keith has been tailing your man all day."

Biscane scoffed lightly. "Bet that's a different gig than Keith is used to."

He thought of the swarthy-featured older wrangler. The man had the patience of Job, so it made sense that they would send him. If he needed to sit in a car outside Jory's office all day, it wouldn't bother the man. On the other hand, even at around the fifty mark, he still had a sharp mind and the reflexes of a much younger man.

"Has Keith reported anything?" Biscane asked, rising to his feet. His bladder twinged, telling him that it was time to start his day . . . with his morning routine.

Still, Biscane needed to hear Gladstone's response.

"According to Keith, Jory spent most of the morning at the courthouse," Gladstone told him. "Lots of security there, so . . . safe. Then he returned to the office and was there all afternoon."

Lludd slid his hand around Archer's waist as he added, "Virgil took Shaw to dinner at a restaurant across the street from Jory's condo complex, and they're watching through the window."

Biscane knew Virgil was a cougar shifter with fantastic instincts. His mate, Shaw, also had heightened survival instincts since he'd been on the run for over a year from a sadistic beta. Shaw, being a rare omega wombat shifter, had the ability to get pregnant—which he was right then—so both of them would be on high alert. If anything was to happen, Biscane knew the pair would see it coming a mile away.

My mate is safe. Now I just need to see him.

While Biscane hadn't made definite plans to see Jory that evening, he couldn't resist going to him. He needed to touch him, hold him, and reassure himself that his human was well. If the gods were with him, perhaps they would even begin their bond, too.

Jory had seemed open to it the prior evening, willing to talk about it at least, and he hoped that desire continued to build as the erotic dreams he knew Fate sent human mates continued to build.

Gods, I want to explore every dream Jory has. I hope he's willing to tell me some day.

"Okay, I gotta go see him," Biscane claimed, heading toward the ensuite. "If there's more, text it to me."

Gladstone scoffed. "You got it. We'll have a meal ready for you to take."

"Thanks!" Biscane called as he closed the door.

Less than thirty minutes later, Biscane was driving one of the ranch's trucks toward town. He wore a large trench coat and gloves to hide his wings and swarthy skin. Keeping his hat pulled low shielded his face. Plus, with the truck window's light tinting and the darkness outside, few would be able to see into the cab.

"Remember not to speed," Spieron had teased with a wink. "It wouldn't be good for you to get pulled over, now would it?"

Anticipation thrummed through him, and he tapped his forefingers restlessly on the wheel. He'd thought about texting Jory, but he didn't want to give his mate a chance to say he was too busy. Instead, he wanted to surprise him with a fantastic dinner for two.

It soothed his base instincts to care for his mate.

It didn't matter that Pauline had actually made the dinner. All that mattered was that Biscane was taking it to him. He would be spreading the food before his mate and getting to watch him eat it.

Hope he's hungry.

Biscane figured eight-thirty at night was a bit later than Jory probably normally ate, not that he'd said anything about it the prior evening, but with spring making the days longer, it was the soonest he could get to his human.

Unless we bond and I go through molt. Then I'll be able to be with him all day and night.

The thought of bonding had a predictable reaction on his cock. He hardened in the jeans he was wearing, and he reached down to adjust himself. Even knowing that most gargoyles became comfortable in the restrictive material eventually, he didn't know how it was possible.

Maybe I'll try slacks next, since my human is a lawyer and always seems to be dressed nicely.

Reaching the city, Biscane focused on driving . . . and keeping his chin tipped down so his hat hid his face. The streets and sidewalks became busy with other traffic.

He made his way through the streets to the downtown

high-rise district. When Attain had heard where Jory lived, he'd whistled under his breath. Evidently, his mate's digs were almost the best a guy could get in the area.

Biscane had felt a rush of irrational pride upon learning his mate was doing so well.

Bypassing the underground parking structure built beneath the seventeen-story building, Biscane drove three blocks away. He parked behind the same fenced-off area he had the prior evening. The place was a construction site that backed up to a shorter high rise.

Claude and Spieron had checked the place out on Sunday, giving Biscane details on how to get to his mate's veranda while avoiding any security cameras. After leaving his coat on the passenger seat and locking up the vehicle, Biscane used that knowledge once more. He easily jumped the fence, then scaled the exterior of the building. Reaching the far corner of the roof, he spread his wings and flew higher.

Landing on a dark corner of Jory's veranda, Biscane felt a niggle of disappointment that his mate wasn't outside waiting as he had been the night before. He pushed it aside, since his human hadn't known he was coming. Moving to the door and placing the satchel he carried on the ground, Biscane rapped on it lightly. After a moment, he did it a second time.

Damn. Hope he's in.

Then Biscane's keen eyesight allowed him to spot movement within the dim interior near the hallway. A living room light flipped on, causing Biscane to squint. He smiled upon seeing his mate, and hunger for something other than food tightened his gut.

Jory was wearing a pair of comfortable sweatpants, which rode low on his hips. His long-sleeved sleep-shirt fitted to his body, accentuating his strong, lean lines. Even his bare feet were sexy. The reading glasses Jory had perched on his head completed the outfit of relaxed comfort.

Biscane grinned, resting his palm on the glass of the French door. To his pleasure, even while appearing surprised, Jory hurried toward him. He unlocked the door and pulled it open.

"Biscane, hi," Jory greeted. His cheeks sported a little pink as he glanced down at himself, which caused the glasses on his head to fall forward back onto his nose. Taking them off and setting them on a side table, he murmured, "Sorry. I wasn't expecting you."

"I was going to give you another day to decompress," Biscane told him as he moved into the house and shut the door behind him. Then he eased into Jory's space and rested his hands on his hips. "But I couldn't stay away from you. I hope I'm not interrupting."

"Just catching up on the endless files," Jory replied, lifting his hands, then hesitating, as if he wasn't certain what to do with them. "It's what I do most nights." He grimaced. "Because I don't really have a life, so somehow I became all work and no play."

"Hmmm, that makes Jory a very dull boy," Biscane rumbled gruffly, teasing his thumb under the edge of his mate's shirt so he could skim over the soft skin of his hipbone. "I brought food." Lifting his other hand, Biscane gently gripped Jory's hands, since he still didn't seem to know what to do with them. He pressed them to his own chest, shivering a little upon feeling his human's hands on him for the first time. "But I find I'm hungry for other things."

Jory cleared his throat. "Well, I did already eat dinner." His cheeks darkened further as he murmured, "Sorry. I didn't know you were coming."

Biscane shook his head once as he rubbed his palm over the back of Jory's hands on his chest before moving it back to his hip. "I understand. I brought a dessert that would be great to eat in bed." Biscane knew he was pushing, but he couldn't seem to help himself . . . not with a rumpled and sexy Jory in his arms. "If you're into that sort of thing."

"I most definitely am," Jory replied huskily. His eyelids lowered to half-mast as he added, "But maybe we can eat that after I've worked up a little appetite first."

Groaning, Biscane nodded eagerly. "I can help with that."

"Good." Then Jory pulled from his grip, only to grab his hand and begin leading him deeper into his home.

Chapter Nine

Jory knew he was thinking with his dick, but the relief he'd felt upon seeing Biscane standing on the other side of his French doors had been tremendous. Seeing his legs encased in form-fitting jeans, the fly cupping his generous package, had been mouthwatering. Then to feel Biscane's rough hands teasing at the skin of his hips — spine-tingling.

In that instant, Jory could think of only one thing . . . to have those hands all over his body.

Leading Biscane to his bedroom, Jory glanced over his shoulder at the male. He saw the hungry gleam in the dark gargoyle's eyes, and a shiver of pride pulsed through him. The male wanted him and had no qualms about showing it.

Taking a page from the gargoyle's book, Jory allowed his own lust to show in his expression as he swept his gaze up and down the male. His swarthy skin was black as night. While his eyes were the same, they appeared to gleam with some inner light. Jory wanted to thread his fingers through his thick black hair and tug it loose from whatever bound it. He loved the feel of hair sliding over his skin, since he had so little, and appreciated the fact that Biscane had long hair.

"With the way you're looking at me," Biscane started, a low growl in his voice. "I'm going to end up rending those clothes from your body and ravishing every inch of you."

Goose bumps broke out on Jory's skin, and the hairs on his arms stood on end. His gut clenched, and he sucked in a swift breath.

"Y-You say that as if it should be a deterrent," Jory pointed out. "But it's not." Having never been a passive lover, and not intending to start with the gargoyle, he gripped the hem of his shirt. "However, since I do like these clothes . . ."

Jory yanked his shirt over his head, peeling it from his body. After tossing it on the box at the foot of the bed, he slid his thumbs into the waistband of his sweats. He hesitated for a heartbeat, wondering if he was ready for what he knew would be coming.

Then Jory spotted the hungry need, the gleam of anticipation and appreciation, in Biscane's eyes, and he reveled in that look.

Yeah. I'm ready.

Before meeting Biscane, a relationship hadn't even been a blip on Jory's radar. After just a few days of texts and Biscane bringing him meals and showing him thoughtful affection, he realized how lonely, how empty his life was. He wanted, *deserved*, more out of life than just work.

Pushing the sweats down his legs, Jory bent and pushed them off. He picked them up and draped them over the box, too. Then Jory faced Biscane, resting his hands on his hips.

While Jory didn't have as many muscles as Biscane, he kept himself in fit shape. He knew he didn't have anything to be ashamed of in the body department. Besides, the way Biscane was staring at him as if he were his own personal dessert bolstered his confidence to a whole new level.

"So, I think someone is overdressed," Jory stated boldly.

Biscane swallowed so hard his Adam's apple bobbed. "Jory." He whispered his name as if it was a benediction. "I-If I undress, I'm going to take you," he warned. "I'm going to tease your flesh with my claws as I lick every inch of your body." His nostrils flared as if he were thinking about just that, and it excited him. Biscane's focus dropped to Jory's straining erection. "Then I'm going to suck your dick as I open your chute. I'm going to drink your seed and relax you before sinking my cock deep into your body and driving you out of your mind with pleasure all over again."

While Jory still felt a little leery about the whole dick up his ass thing, he knew he would get a chance at Biscane's, too. Attain had told him that bonding went both ways. Plus, gargoyles were hardwired to please their mate, so if Jory didn't end up liking it, he wouldn't have to do it again.

Although, Jory liked the sound of everything else Biscane said he would do, and considering the gargoyle was almost a thousand years old — something he'd been shocked to learn during their conversation over dinner the previous evening — he bet the gargoyle knew what he was doing and how to please a lover.

After all, LeeAnn became fixated on him.

"It's okay," Biscane began softly, easing a step toward him. "I'll just stay mostly dressed. It'll help me stay in control. I—"

Realizing his silence had given Biscane the wrong idea — and that thoughts of Biscane's crazy stalker had no place in the bedroom — Jory reached for the gargoyle. "Sorry. The way you look at me leaves me tongue-tied," Jory told Biscane as he reached for the fly of his jeans. "I want these off, and I want everything you just promised." As he flipped the button and carefully lowered his new lover's zipper, he stated, "I've never been with a man."

"I'll take ever-so-good care of you, Jory," Biscane told him, his words sounding like a vow. "You are the other half of my soul, and I can't wait to spend the rest of my days fulfilling every one of your needs."

Jory countered, "That goes both ways, Biscane. I don't want this to be a one-sided relationship."

Biscane immediately nodded. "I understand." Cradling Jory's jaw in one hand, he dipped his head. "And I love that about you."

Before Jory could respond — *holy shit, did he just say he loves me* — Biscane pressed his lips to Jory's. He gasped in surprise, shocked at the sensations the simple contact sent through him. With the way Biscane's sharp canines peeked over his lips, Jory hadn't thought the male would be able to kiss . . . but boy was he pleased to learn he was wrong.

Taking advantage of Jory's slightly parted lips, Biscane eased his tongue between them. He used his hold on Jory's face while tipping his head to the side, deepening the kiss. Delving deep, he mapped Jory's mouth, teasing along his tongue and gliding along his teeth.

Jory grabbed Biscane's upper arms and did a little exploring of his own. Dueling with the gargoyle's tongue, he discovered it was a little longer and narrower than he was used to. The knowledge allowed him to suckle lightly on the appendage, drawing a deep groan from Biscane.

Finally, when Jory's lungs screamed for air, he turned his head and broke the kiss. He swept his gaze over Biscane's face and torso, pleased to see him panting, telling him he wasn't the only one out of breath. Grinning, Jory winked, then peered down at the gargoyle's open fly . . . and the jeans that still clung to his hips.

Oh, and the huge shaft jutting between the flaps. Holy shit, how the hell am I going to take that?

Upon seeing the impressive, probably ten-inch cock, Jory couldn't tear his gaze away. He couldn't control how his breathing sped up or the way his ass clenched. His heart rate ratcheted up for a new reason.

He's massive!

"Easy, Jory," Biscane purred. Using a crooked finger under his chin, he urged him to lift his focus and meet his gaze. "I know I'm big, but you'll be able to take me. I promise. I'll use every trick I know to relax you, to minimize the pain of your first breach." With a heated smile curving his lips, Biscane told him, "I will play with your body until you're writhing in passion, my mate."

Jory knew he had to have faith in Biscane, or their relation-ship would never work. Forcing a nod, he whispered, "I trust you."

Biscane grinned widely, beaming with pleasure. "Grab the lube and lie on the bed, Jory," he urged as he took a step back-ward, releasing him.

Turning to his bed, Jory grabbed the comforter and yanked it to the foot of the bed. He pushed back the sheet a bit before opening his nightstand. With the advent of the erotic dreams — which Attain told him was part of Fate urging him to accept Biscane — he'd bought a bottle of lube. Grabbing it, Jory placed it on the nightstand.

Then Jory crawled onto the bed and flopped onto his back. He pushed his feet under the top sheet but didn't bother pull-ing it up. Focusing on Biscane, he groaned appreciatively at the sight before him — the huge black gargoyle naked in all his glory.

And what a sight to behold.

Biscane's thick muscles rippled under his hide as he stalked forward. His huge black wings billowed in the air be-hind him. He licked his full lips as a rumbling growl erupted from him.

"Soooo gorgeous," Biscane growled. "My gorgeous lawyer mate." Resting one knee on the bed, then the other, his cock swung obscenely as he crawled on the bed. "Want to play with your beautiful body for hours on end."

Jory trembled in anticipation. His dick, which had softened a little with his nerves, roared back to life with a vengeance. Hard and throbbing, it tapped against his stomach insistently.

"Mmmm, you do like that idea," Biscane crooned softly. "Excellent."

Sitting back on his calves, Biscane rested one hand on Jory's chest, rubbing a thumb and a finger over each nipple, causing it to bead and his breath to catch. He bent the fingers of his other hand and skimmed the backs of his claws up Jory's straining erection. The light touch from those dangerous appendages caused his breath to catch in his chest and heat to bloom through his groin. A bead of pre-cum oozed from his tip.

Biscane hummed as he scooped it up with a forefinger. With a wicked grin, he brought it to his lips and sucked it from his digit. He smacked his lips exaggeratedly as he tasted him.

"Delicious," Biscane claimed. "Can't wait to taste more of you."

Before Jory could respond, Biscane levered over him. He replaced his thumb with his lips, wrapping them around his nipple and sucked. With his other hand, he began lightly pinching and plucking at his other nub.

Jory had never considered his nipples sensitive, but what Biscane was doing set his blood on fire. His buds contracted and tingled, spreading zings of sensation across his skin. He arched, twisting his fingers into the sheet beneath him as he groaned loudly.

Biscane hummed in response, but he didn't stop. Instead, he rested his other hand on Jory's torso and began mapping his body. He scraped his nails along the outline of his ribs, dipped into his belly button, then teased over his hip bones.

Shudders racked Jory as he gave him over to the sensations caused by Biscane's touches. His toes even curled as his body bowed. He couldn't help the way his legs moved restlessly on the sheet, his body beyond his control.

Tipping his head back, Jory moaned Biscane's name as he felt his balls begin to tighten without even another touch to his dick.

When Biscane popped off his nipple, he grinned down at him. "Gods, I love how you respond, my mate," he rumbled. "Like my perfect dream."

Before Jory could complain at the loss of stimulation, Biscane shoved the sheet off his feet. Then he gripped his calf and pushed his legs wider. When Biscane moved between his legs, seeing the other man there, a gasp of nerves burst from Jory's chest.

"Relax," Biscane purred. Then he winked and rumbled, "Or don't."

Jory's aroused mind couldn't process what Biscane meant. Except, then the gargoyle gripped the base of his dick. He lifted up as he bent over, opened his mouth, and swallowed his erection to the root.

Crying out with delight, Jory bucked. Wet heat and sucking pressure shorted out his brain. His gut clenched, and his limbs tensed as his orgasm threatened.

Before Jory could gather enough brain cells to warn Biscane, his release crashed over him. His balls tightened pleasantly as his gut clenched. With a spine-tingling throb, his erection poured burst after burst of cum into Biscane's mouth.

Biscane swallowed it all, licking along his length, continuing to tease his sensitive flesh. Moving one hand between Jory's legs, he gently pressed against his prostate from the outside, stimulating his gland. He scraped his claws over his torso, touching him everywhere.

Jory floated on the endorphins from the best release of his life. Sighing deeply, he relaxed against his comforter as he drifted pleasantly. He managed to peel one hand from the sheet and threaded his fingers into Biscane's hair, needing to touch the gargoyle.

Peering at Jory through his lashes, Biscane met his gaze. He finally pulled off his spent dick long enough to smile and say, "Delectable, my mate." Then Biscane began lapping lightly at Jory's flared head, sending fresh zings through his groin.

As Jory relaxed, reveling in Biscane's continued touches, he watched the gargoyle reach over and grab the lube. He knew what the male was planning to do, but his mind was too re-laxed to care. When Biscane pushed Jory's left leg up and out, spreading him wide, he didn't offer any resistance.

Jory also couldn't summon up any nerves, either.

Biscane was too busy continuing to play with his body, touching, teasing, and massaging every inch of his skin from his nipples to his thighs. The continued lapping, sucking, and nuzzles on his cock kept his body simmering with arousal. When Biscane lowered his head and sucked a ball into his mouth, Jory groaned, his eyes almost rolling to the back of his head.

"Biscane," Jory slurred, too blissed-out to care. "So good."

His gargoyle lover popped off his testicle just long enough to murmur, "Love taking care of you," before returning to driving Jory out of his mind.

CHAPTER TEN

Biscane reveled in the blissed-out expression on Jory's face. The way his mate moved into his touches, silently searching for more, caused his blood to burn. How the human gave himself over to Biscane's ministrations, trusting him implicitly, was the greatest gift he could ever have been given.

And I will never do anything to jeopardize it.

With that in mind, Biscane poured a liberal amount of lube onto the fingers of his right hand. He knew his forever love had never done anything like this before, and he had every intention of making certain Jory enjoyed the experience. His instinct to please demanded that it be so.

As Biscane teased his slick finger over Jory's muscled opening, massaging the tight entrance, he continued to suckle on Jory's flared crown. With his other hand, he gently fondled the soft folds of his ball sack. He'd been oh-so-pleasantly surprised to discover just how sensitive his mate's genitals were.

Gonna use that to distract the ever-loving hell out of him.

Doing just that, Biscane licked, nipped, and sucked all over his mate's cock and balls. He nuzzled, hummed, and scraped, switching up the stimulation often. Keeping his focus on Jory's face and chest, cataloging the way he moaned, whimpered, twitched, and shuddered, Biscane kept him so distracted, his mate didn't even flinch when he finally added a fourth finger.

Biscane knew he was a big man, and he had no intention of hurting his mate.

Once Jory took all four of his fingers easily, even rocking

into his gentle thrusts, Biscane lifted his face from his mate's groin. "You're ready, my mate," he rumbled, loving his human's heavy-lidded expression and flushed features. "First time's easiest on your stomach." Biscane touched his fingertips to Jory's prostate lightly, keeping him on edge. "Would you like to roll over?"

For a few seconds, Jory remained silent. He licked his lips and swallowed. Then his brows furrowed.

Biscane worried Jory would deny him for one heartbeat, two . . . until his mate smiled up at him.

"Like this," Jory decided. "I want to see your face."

Returning Jory's smile, Biscane nodded. "I'll be careful."

He eased his fingers free of Jory's chute. Hearing his lover's whine of dismay, he grinned and quickly replaced it with his tail, keeping up the internal pressure. Grabbing a pillow in one hand, he wrapped his other arm under Jory's ass and gently lifted.

Once Biscane had the pillow beneath Jory's hips, he levered over him. He stared into his mate's eyes for several seconds, enjoying the mixture of relaxation and expectation in his gaze. Dipping his head, Biscane pressed his lips to Jory's, beginning a slow, thorough — and distracting — kiss.

At the same time, Biscane felt around for the lube. He found it, then poured some onto his erection by feel, knowing he was probably making a mess of the sheets, too, but he would deal with it later. Biscane closed the lube and tossed it aside before gripping his dick, coating it fully with the slick, and guiding it to his lover's stretched hole.

Biscane continued to manipulate Jory's mouth and tongue as he pulled his tail free. Touching his sensitive cock head to his mate's hole pulled a soft growl from his chest. He pushed, breaching Jory's muscled ring. Using patience born of centuries, Biscane oh-so-slowly sank into the most exquisite heat he'd ever experienced.

Unable to help himself, Biscane broke the kiss. He groaned loudly as a shudder worked through his body. Bottoming out in Jory's tight, wet sheath was the most erotic moment of his life. He sucked in a few deep breaths, struggling for control.

"I'm okay," Jory whispered roughly. "You can move."

Jory wrapped his arms around Biscane and rubbed them up and down the sides of his back.

While Biscane knew Jory meant to soothe, his mate's touch enflamed his senses to a fever pitch instead. His desire to rut, to ream his human's tight, glorious body caused his gut to clench. A shudder worked through him as he lifted his head and met Jory's gaze.

"Stay still, my mate," Biscane ordered with a growl. Upon seeing the way Jory's brows shot up and scenting his surprise, he soothed, "I don't wish to hurt you, and it's taking every ounce of self-control I have not to rut to completion." Sliding one arm under Jory to grip his shoulder from behind, Biscane rubbed his other palm down his human's side. "I want this to be a pleasurable experience, Jory. Perfect."

Curving his lips into a warm smile, Jory told him, "How about we strive for perfection another day, Biscane. I'm about ready to blow again, and I want to feel your dick sliding over my prostate over and over." Once more, Jory rubbed over Biscane's hide. "Make me come again." He narrowed his eyes. "You promised."

Growling softly, Biscane grinned upon hearing the playfulness in Jory's tone. "I did promise," he confirmed. Lowering his head, he whispered into his mate's ear. "And I will always deliver on my promises."

Then Biscane began to move. Upon feeling Jory's muscles ripple along his length, he let out a heartfelt moan of pleasure. As soon as his lover's muscle tugged at the edges of his swollen crown, Biscane reversed direction and began sinking in again.

So deep. So good.

Biscane did his best to keep it slow, but after a few thrust and retreats, his control dwindled. Speeding up, faster and faster with each repetition, he lost himself in the exquisite bliss of having his mate in his arms, under him and surrounding him. He could think of nothing that would ever feel as amazing as loving his human, the other half of his soul.

In an embarrassingly short period of time, Biscane felt his balls begin to tighten. His body shuddered as he pounded into Jory over and over. He reveled in hearing the low groans, cries, and moans escaping his mate's lips.

When Biscane knew he could put off his release no longer, he reached between them and gripped Jory's cock. He jacked his lover's dick, enjoying the smooth, hard flesh in his hand. His mate's cries dwindled to low grunts of masculine pleasure, telling Biscane how close he was.

With one more swift stroke while nailing Jory's prostate, Biscane heard his lover's cry of completion. He felt his mate's chute muscles clamp onto his cock, and he buried himself as deep as possible and froze. The slightly salty scent of Jory's seed filled the air, making his mouth water for another taste.

Biscane's body's need rose up and crashed over him like the best kind of tidal wave. Endorphins flooded his system, sending him swimming in ecstasy. Crying Jory's name, he clutched his mate tight against him and reveled in every pinging bit of pleasure.

With his instincts driving him, Biscane opened his mouth. He wrapped his mouth around the point of Jory's shoulder. Unable to stop himself, even if he'd wanted to, he bit.

The flavor of Jory's iron-rich blood coated his tongue as his life-fluid flowed into his mouth. After swallowing that mouthful, he sucked on the wound, moaning with delight. For several long heartbeats, he could focus on nothing but the heady goodness of drinking his mate's essence.

The feel of Jory shuddering beneath him finally penetrated

Biscane's senses. He eased his teeth free and swallowed before licking over the wound. Cleaning every trace of Jory's blood while sealing his bite, Biscane hummed appreciatively at the claiming mark he revealed.

When Biscane shifted his focus to Jory's face, smug satisfaction filled him. His mate's lips were curved in a smile of pure satisfaction. His eyes were closed, and he snored softly.

Biscane sighed as he eased out of Jory's body, ignoring his still-hard dick. Until they completely finished their bond, he would remain aroused if he was around his mate. His mate, however, seemed to need sleep, instead of more sex.

He did say multiple orgasms were beyond his body's age. Perhaps this is what he meant.

Settling against his mate's side, Biscane propped his head up on one hand. He used his other hand to tease at the few gray strands gracing Jory's temples. They gave him a distinguished look which Biscane found fascinating.

"I would love to put you to sleep like this every night," Biscane whispered. Unable to help himself, he slid his hand down and lightly fingered the scar his bite had left behind. Pride filled him that every paranormal would now know that Jory was his.

Jory moaned softly as he shifted a little in his sleep.

Biscane pulled his hand away. After pecking a kiss to Jory's temple, he carefully eased from the bed. He headed toward a half-open door, spotting the edge of a sink inside.

Once inside the bathroom with the door nearly closed, Biscane flipped on the light. He grabbed a washcloth and soaked it in warm water. After he'd cleaned himself, hissing softly at the feel of the cloth sliding over his sensitive rod, Biscane ran the cloth under the water again.

He'd just begun rinsing the cloth so he could take it to Jory when the door opened wider. Seeing his naked mate in the doorway, he smiled and swept his gaze over the man appreciatively. Some possessive part of himself that he'd never before experienced reared its head as he spotted his seed coating Jory's inner thighs.

"Gods, you're sexy," Biscane blurted.

"And dirty," Jory added, glancing down at himself wryly. "Can't believe you knocked me out with orgasms." Lifting a hand, he stopped himself before touching his neck. "Attain said the bite was orgasmic, but I must admit, I had a hard time believing him."

Biscane chuckled softly as he wrung out the washcloth. "I heard it's hard for humans to believe unless they experience it." Then he held up the cloth. "I was coming back to clean you." Then, remembering how much lube he'd used, Biscane added, "And to change the sheets."

"I already stripped them," Jory admitted, grimacing as he peered over his shoulder. "I normally leave my laundry for a service, but leaving those for them, well—"

Jory rubbed the back of his neck, which was a big enough admittance of unease even without the slight embarrassment in his scent.

"If it's a cleaning service, I'm quite certain they'll have seen plenty worse than a little extra lube and some semen," Biscane pointed out. When Jory still didn't relax, he lowered to his knees before his human. "However, if it's that big of a concern for you"—as he spoke, he began gently clearing away the semen from his mate's stomach—"I can take your sheets to the ranch and wash them there."

"That makes me sound like a prude, doesn't it," Jory whispered, standing still—albeit a bit tense—for Biscane's ministrations. "It's just—"

When Jory didn't finish, Biscane glanced up from what he was doing and paused. "You've never brought someone home before, have you?"

Jory shook his head.

Biscane grinned broadly, unable to help himself. "I'm the only other person who's ever been in that bed, aren't I?"

While Biscane hadn't scented anyone else, he hadn't wanted to jump to conclusions. After all, it could have just been a while. Now he knew differently.

All mine!

"Yes, you are." Jory smirked at him. "And you're incredibly happy about that. Aren't you?"

"I am." Biscane didn't see the point in beating around the bush. Continuing his cleaning ministrations, he stated, "You're mine, and I'm yours. Something about sharing your bed with only you soothes some possessive need in me I never realized I had."

Cocking his head, Jory whispered, "I suppose you couldn't say the same about that for your bed."

Biscane snapped his focus from Jory's half-hard prick where he was wiping away the last traces of their fluids. Seeing his human's narrowed eyes, he knew what the man was thinking. He needed to nip that idea in the bud damn quick . . . which reminded him that they hadn't done any talking or sharing of information before they'd tumbled into bed.

"Jory, I don't have a bed," Biscane told him. Upon seeing his mate's eyes widen in surprise, he explained, "I'm a stone statue during the day. I work at a cattle ranch. I roost in a barn." With a grin, Biscane asked, "You remember the cot you woke up on with me Saturday night?"

Jory nodded. "Yeah."

Biscane admitted, "Nicholas put a number of those in the loft when we first arrived at the ranch, and we all got a kick out of it." Chuckling quietly, he grinned at his lover. "We're a stone statue during the day, so what do we care if we sleep on a bed or crouch on the roof of a church or a castle."

Chuckling, Jory nodded. "Got it." He held his gaze as he asked, "So, have you ever had a bed?"

"When I lived in a clutch several hundred years ago, I had

my own suite of rooms," Biscane told Jory as he rose to his feet. "I had a bed there, and I used it to fuck." After tossing the soiled cloth in a dirty clothes basket, he explained, "When I became an enforcer for the gargoyle elders, I left that clutch behind. I also stopped taking people to my bed." Realizing how that sounded, Biscane quickly amended, "What I mean is, I always went to their bed, or there wasn't a bed involved. Um—"

Jory slapped his hand over Biscane's mouth. "You should stop while you're ahead."

Fortunately, he was staring at him with amusement.

Biscane kissed Jory's stomach before rising to his feet. "Now then, why don't we put new sheets on your bed, grab that dessert I told you about, and stretch out on the bed?" Giving his mate an encouraging smile, he told him, "We do have a couple of things to discuss before we talk about how you want to fuck me so we can complete our bond."

Licking his lips, Jory stared up at him as heat filled his eyes. "I like that idea very much."

Grinning, Biscane pecked a kiss to Jory's lips. Then he guided him back to the bedroom so they could do just that.

CHAPTER ELEVEN

The sound of soft, pain-filled grunts and hisses roused Jory from a sound sleep. Blinking open his gum-filled eyes, he realized he must not have been asleep for long—or nearly long enough. His sluggish mind recognized the dim light coming between the blinds as the first rays of dawn.

Damn, I called in sick so I didn't have to deal with this fatigue headache.

Jory heard another hiss and frowned. "Biscane?" he rasped. Hours of groaning and calling out his lover's name meant he really needed some water to soothe his vocal cords before he would begin to sound normal.

"I-It's fine." Biscane's deep voice held a definite note of strain to it. "Sorry I woke you."

"What's wrong?" Jory could hear it in Biscane's voice. Plus, the arm around his torso and the big body pressed against his back felt tense. As Jory eased to his back, he felt a completely unfamiliar tell-tale twinge in his chute, reminding him of their bliss-inducing and energetic activities . . . for most of the evening. "Talk to me. Did something we did hurt you?"

Finally able to see Biscane's face, Jory easily spotted the lines of pain there. He continued to roll until he faced the gargoyle. Resting his hands on his lover's shoulders, he urged him to lie on his back, which he did with a wince.

"Tell me," Jory demanded, levering up on an elbow and peering down at him. "What's going on?" That was when Jory's tired brain registered something else. "It's dawn. Are you turning to stone?"

"Molt," Biscane bit out through gritted teeth. "The first change is painful." He swallowed hard before adding, "It'll pass."

"Molt," Jory whispered, recalling that word. "The first change."

Biscane nodded.

"Is there anything I can do to help?"

Wrapping his arms around Jory, Biscane pulled him close. "Sprawl on me, mate," he urged.

As odd as the request was, Jory went with it. He half-lay on Biscane's chest. Hearing the gargoyle's sigh and feeling some of his tension ease, Jory rubbed over his side and neck with his hands. That seemed to soothe Biscane even more.

Jory shuffled to the side a little, testing a theory, until he was completely covering Biscane. If the male hadn't been so huge, he never would have tried it. He didn't consider himself a small man, and he would never risk smooshing a lover. With Biscane, Jory knew he never needed to worry about that.

"Nice," Biscane whispered. "Thank you."

Flushing himself against Biscane's front, Jory's toes barely reached the base of his calves. He rested his chin on the left side of his lover's shoulder. Jory roved his hands over every other inch of exposed flesh as he listened to Biscane's breathing hitch, his soft grunts, and his stifled hisses.

When Biscane's back bowed and he arched beneath Jory, he nearly tumbled off the gargoyle. Only his lover's tight bands around his waist and torso held him in place. A second later, to Jory's astonishment, Biscane's wings appeared to retract somewhere beneath him, disappearing from sight.

Jory continued to stare in awe as Biscane's skin tone lightened considerably and smoothed out. His angular jaw eased a little as his teeth lost their pointedness and no longer peeked over his full lips. The frame he lay on seemed to lose some of its bulk, and if the way his toes now touched the tops of his lover's feet, he'd lost some height, too.

Finally, Jory found himself lying on a man who appeared to be of mixed heritage with light-brown skin and long black hair.

Reaching up, Jory threaded his fingers through that hair, reveling in the fact that his lover still had it. He loved touching Biscane's hair. After Jory had been petting the male for a few seconds, Biscane opened his eyes—eyes still as dark as night—and smiled up at him tentatively.

Jory recalled Attain's comment about how gargoyles' sense of attraction differed from humans. They appreciated all body types and were more interested in the way someone smelled. Most paranormals tended to steer clear of those who used chemicals or overpowering perfumes or colognes.

"That means, after going through molt, they're gonna need a little confidence boost," Attain had told him. *"They'll need to know that you care about him in either form, not favoring one over the other."*

With how serious Attain had sounded when he'd told him, Jory knew it was important.

Smiling down at his gargoyle in human form, Jory continued to thread his fingers through his hair as he told him, "You have no idea how much I love getting to slide my fingers through your hair. I'm so glad it's still long when you look human." With a wink, Jory added, "I hope you intend to keep it loose unless you're working."

Biscane's smile lost its uncertainty. "For you, anything."

"This is a good look for you," Jory commented idly, sliding to Biscane's side so he could take in the whole picture of the man lying next to him. He still had considerable bulk, which seemed to be a common theme for gargoyles in their human form. "When I take you to dinner and show you off, I'm going to have to stick close to your side, or someone is going to try to steal you from me."

"No one will ever be able to steal me," Biscane countered,

his arms tightening around Jory and holding him close. "We're bonded." Nuzzling his temple, he whispered, "I'm yours, and you're mine, Jory. I look forward to using the next several hundred years to get to know everything about you."

Jory chuckled as he turned his head and accepted a peck to his lips. "I don't think it's going to take that long."

Biscane shrugged one large shoulder, making Jory's head bob. "That's fine, too." A bit of uncertainty once more took hold of his features. "You sure I look okay?"

"*More* than okay," Jory assured. Guessing what Biscane's next fear would be — that Jory might like Biscane better in human form — he did his best to waylay it before it could take root. "Although, I'll definitely miss your wings when we have to go out among human society. Sometime at the ranch, would you take me flying?"

"Really?" Biscane sounded pleased. "You want to go flying with me?"

"Absolutely," Jory confirmed. "I love hang-gliding. Maybe someday we can go somewhere that I can hang-glide while you fly beside me." As soon as the idea popped into his mind, Jory knew he would want to do it some day. "What do you think?"

Biscane took on a stricken look. "Honestly? The idea of you gliding through the air on one of those flimsy contraptions freaks me out."

Jory laughed as he shook his head. "They're not that flimsy. They're made of aluminum alloy and this type of strong, light plastic that —"

When Biscane settled his hand over Jory's mouth and shook his head while sporting wide eyes, he had to laugh again, even if it was muffled behind the male's hand.

"Please don't tell me," Biscane requested, sounding pained for a whole new reason. "It just freaks me out more."

Gripping Biscane's hand, Jory eased it away from his

mouth. "Well, now you'll always be there to catch me," he told him, smiling at him.

"Yes, I will," Biscane vowed.

Jory shifted back onto his elbow and leaned forward, giving Biscane a slow, thorough kiss. As they licked at each other, he realized he hadn't given one thought to morning breath. Smiling at that realization, he continued to map Biscane's human-shaped mouth, amazed to find that he truly missed his gargoyle's sharper teeth.

Lifting his head, Jory panted lightly as he peered at his lover. He couldn't believe the changes to his life in just a few short days. Attain had warned him that paranormals did things fast, but this was even faster than he'd expected.

As Jory took in the expression — *gods, is that love* — on Biscane's features, he knew it was okay by him. A permanent lover, a partner, hadn't even been a blip on his radar. Now that Jory had Biscane, he wouldn't give him up for anything.

Which could make work interesting.

It'll be worth it, though.

Feeling the dampness of the sheet beneath him, Jory took a second to really take in Biscane. His skin gleamed with sweat, and the area around him appeared wet. He realized just how hard on the gargoyle going through molt had been.

Jory found a desire to take care of his lover rise within him. Acting on the unexpected sensation, he began easing away from Biscane. "Come in the shower with me," he urged. "I want to wash you and massage your sore muscles." When Biscane arched one brow in silent question, Jory added, "It looked and sounded painful, and I know you did your best to hide that from me." Standing beside the bed, he held out his hand, palm up. "Give me a chance to pamper you."

Biscane took Jory's hand and allowed him to help him from the bed. "As if I could ever resist an offer like that."

After half an hour in the shower, where Jory took advantage of a naked and wet Biscane and explored every inch of his new body, he eased his softening prick out of his gargoyle's hot, tight channel. Resting his forehead against his lover's back, he rubbed his hand up and down his torso. He sighed deeply as pleasant endorphins pinged through his system from his release.

"Damn, Bis," Jory mumbled before chuckling softly. "Never had shower sex before." After pecking a kiss to his gargoyle's smooth mocha skin, he admitted, "Think I might like to do it again, but with you in your true form. I'll just have to get a box to stand on."

Biscane's rumbling chuckles filled the stall. Turning to peer over his shoulder at him, he revealed twinkling dark eyes. "Anytime, my mate." He rubbed his palm up and down Jory's hip. "Love feeling you move inside me."

Jory's prick gave an appreciative throb when he heard those words, and he groaned softly. "Can't get it up again, yet," he muttered. Then he yawned widely. "Damn, I need some coffee if we're not going back to sleep."

"We can go back to sleep if you wish, Jory." Biscane turned in Jory's embrace, then wrapped his arms around him. Waggling his black brows, he stated, "I know I kept you up all night. While I'm sorry you felt the need to call in sick, I'm not sorry for the reason why."

"I'm not sorry, either," Jory replied. Then he admitted, "And I have so much sick time stored up, I could pretend I had the flu for three weeks and no one would be the wiser."

Biscane shook his head as he eyed him with concern. "You work too much, my mate."

"I do indeed." Jory could admit his shortcomings as he grabbed a towel and began drying Biscane. "Now I have a reason to work on that."

Picking up the second towel from the rack, Biscane tried to

dry Jory, too. When their hands kept bumping and they kept getting in each other's way, Jory laughed and stepped backward. Then he began drying himself. Biscane grinned and did the same.

After that, they returned to the bedroom. Once more, they stripped the sheets. Jory found his last clean set and placed them on the bed. He eyed the two soiled sets and shook his head.

"At this rate, we're going to make a mess out of these before we have a chance to wash the others," Jory teased as he grabbed a pair of sweatpants out of his dresser.

Biscane chuckled. "I can have someone from the ranch pick us up some." Then he sobered as he pulled on his jeans. "As well as some clothes for me. I didn't wear a shirt here, and for some reason, I don't think any of yours will fit me."

"Afraid not," Jory confirmed as he began leading the way out of his room to his kitchen. "And as much as going back to sleep would be nice, my brain doesn't work that way. I'll be awake for at least three hours before my brain will think about shutting back down again," he explained. "I'll make us breakfast, and we can discuss what we want to—"

The chime of his front door made Jory pause. He frowned. "That's odd."

"Odd to have someone visit?" Biscane asked curiously, peering toward the foyer. "You don't get many guests?"

Jory shook his head as he moved slowly toward the front door. "Not that," he admitted. "There's a front desk. I should have been called and asked because I don't have an approved guest list." Pausing, Jory met Biscane's gaze. "Although, I'll add you to it today and get a key for you, too."

Biscane grinned broadly. "Thank you, my mate." Then he sobered and pointed toward the bedroom. "Head to bed, my mate. You're supposed to be sick. I'll handle whoever is here."

Hesitating, Jory scrubbed his hand through his wet hair.

He appreciated that Biscane waited patiently for him to make a decision. Whoever was at the door wasn't so kind. They rang the chime twice more, then pounded on the door.

Rolling his eyes, Jory grumbled, "If they're that impatient, I'm sure I don't want to deal with them." He headed toward the hall leading to the bedroom. "I'll leave the door open so I can hear."

"How should I introduce myself?" Biscane asked, cocking his head.

"My boyfriend," Jory replied without hesitation. Then he grimaced. "That sounds juvenile, doesn't it?"

Biscane beamed at him even as he chuckled, clearly pleased. "I'll take it, my mate. Head to bed."

Jory nodded and returned to the bedroom. Leaving the door open a crack, he leaned against the wall. He wished he'd had time to make a cup of coffee before they'd been interrupted.

Hearing Biscane opening the door caught Jory's attention.

"Can I help you?" Biscane's deep voice rumbled.

"Who are you?" George Walsh's voice demanded. "Where's Jory?"

Well, shit. What's he doing here?

George had never visited Jory before. Even if the man needed files for work—and Jory knew he didn't have any meetings planned that day—the lawyer wouldn't have come himself. Instead, one of their lower paralegals would have been dispatched to get the files.

"Jory called in sick, so he's in bed," Biscane answered, his tone holding a hint of annoyance. "And I'm his boyfriend, not that it's any of your business."

"Actually, it *is* my business," George replied, a sneer in his voice. "I knew when he started visiting that faggot ranch that he'd been tainted. Where is he?" he demanded again. "I can't wait to tell him he's finished."

Deciding that he'd heard enough, Jory grabbed a t-shirt

and pulled it on. In the process, he missed whatever Biscane said in response, but he recognized malicious laughter when he heard it. Jory reached the end of the hall and froze, shock filling him.

George had always appeared put together—dressed impeccably without a hair out of place. The man before him was nothing like that person. His hair stuck up at odd angles as if he'd repeatedly run his hands through it. His jacket was unbuttoned, and he didn't wear a tie. Even his shoes were scuffed, and there was dirt on them.

"George?" Jory called softly, not liking the manic gleam in the other lawyer's brown eyes. "What are you doing here? What's going on?"

Pinning him with a sneer, George pulled a gun from somewhere inside his jacket and pointed it at him. "Your untimely health is just the excuse I need to have you removed from the firm," he stated, suddenly sounding way too calm. "But first, if you want your faggot lover to live, you're going to do something for me. Otherwise"—George swung the gun to point it at Biscane—"he's dead."

Jory's breath caught in his throat as his pulse spiked. "I'll do anything," he vowed, fear permeating him.

I can't lose Biscane now. Not when I just found him.

CHAPTER TWELVE

"I knew you would," George stated coldly. "You fags are so weak."

Biscane barely swallowed the growl that threatened to erupt from his throat. When he'd peered through the peep-hole, he hadn't recognized the human. When he'd let him in, his underlying scent had reminded him of Attain, telling him that the older man was a relation.

Then Jory had come into the room, and all had become clear.

This is Attain's asshole, homophobic father . . . and it looks as if he's gone round the bend.

Seeing George pull a gun and point it at Jory had damn near caused Biscane's heart to stop in his chest. Then . . . the moron had pointed it at him. As much as Biscane loved the way Jory had vowed to do anything to save him, he knew he wouldn't need to.

As long as the gun stays pointed at me . . . except, I need to know a few things.

"Why are you doing this?" Biscane demanded, although he didn't raise his hands. "We haven't done anything to you."

Scoffing, George curled his lip as he looked him up and down. "Look at you. Six-foot-six of pure muscle, and you're willing to take it up the ass. What a disgusting disgrace of a human being," he rambled, shaking his head in disgust. "If it was up to me, I'd kill every single one of you." While George peered at Jory, he didn't change who he pointed the gun at.

Good.

"But I'm willing to settle for a trade," George claimed.

"What kind of trade?" Jory asked quietly.

Biscane could scent Jory's fear, and he hated the acrid aroma. For the first time in his centuries-long-life, he wished he was a vampire. A vampire could speak to his bonded beloved telepathically. Biscane would have been able to mentally reassure his lover.

Instead, Biscane could only stay calm, offer his mate a reassuring persona, and wait for his opening.

"Bring me Attain," George demanded. "I won't have my son cavorting with those faggots any longer." Then he growled under his breath, "If that damn wrangler hadn't gotten distracted by some guy, she could have done it. Women are so worthless."

Huh. At least he's an equal opportunity hater. Wait. Woman?

"Attain lives there with his partner," Jory pointed out. "He's happy there."

"I don't care!" George screamed, swinging his arm to point the gun at Jory. "He'll do as I say or die!"

Jory lifted his hands in placation, his back stiffening as his eyes rounded. "Uh, okay."

George's eyes turned a little vacant as he mumbled, "After I deal with my son, I'll finish clearing out the rest of the riff-raff at my firm." Snorting, he wiggled his gun at Jory, adding, "You'll have to retire, of course. I'll find a way to get rid of Reginald, too. He's too old and apathetic."

"Wait." Jory's voice came out soft, sounding confused even. "Is that why you've been so mean to some of the interns, paralegals, and lawyers?" His eyes narrowed, and it was obvious to Biscane that he was trying to work something out. "You're trying to remove the"—he paused and cleared his throat—"riff-raff from the office?"

Scoffing, George smirked. "For being a lawyer, you sure are slow on the uptake."

Needing to get the gun pointed back at him, Biscane

snorted as he narrowed his eyes. "Soooo, you're the one who's been paying off LeeAnn."

"How did you know about that?" George demanded, admitting to his bribery by his word choice.

Biscane smirked, curving his lips in a pleased smile. "Because I'm the one who distracted her from your goal." Grinning widely, he rested his fists on his hips. "But she didn't have what it took to keep my interest. Who wants tits and a pussy when you can have a nice tight ass and hard dick?"

Just as Biscane had hoped, George swung the gun back toward him. "Such vile filth," he roared. His hand trembled as his face turned red. "If I didn't need you alive—"

"But you didn't need LeeAnn alive, did you?" Biscane interrupted, doing his best to goad the man. He needed him just a little more off-kilter. "You're the one who killed her, aren't you?" He swept his gaze up and down the human's frame. While a little heavier than Attain, he was just as tall and appeared to have plenty of muscle. "She told you she couldn't work at the ranch anymore, and since she knew what you were trying to do, kidnap your own son, you killed her. Didn't you?"

"Yeah, I did," George admitted without a hint of remorse in sight. "Just like I'm gonna kill you."

Biscane saw George's arm straighten. Diving to the left, he rolled across the hardwood floor. He bounced back to his feet and launched at Attain's father.

As a gargoyle, Biscane was far faster than any human could ever hope to be. He was on the man in seconds. Grabbing George's wrist, Biscane took their attacker to the condo's hardwood floor.

Hearing George's head smack against the floor and hearing the gun sliding across it, Biscane wasn't at all surprised to see Attain's father out cold. He checked for a pulse, found it strong, and tried to decide if that was okay with him.

"Biscane?"

Hearing Jory's uncertain, trembling voice, Biscane dismissed the downed man. He jumped to his feet and took in his mate. He didn't like the way his lover stared at him with wide eyes or the way trembles racked him.

Biscane lifted his hands, palms out, and murmured, "I'm fine, Jory. Just fine." He took a step toward his mate, hoping his lover would welcome him after seeing him perpetrate such violence. "Are you?"

For a few seconds, Jory just stared at him with wide eyes. Then he cried, "Am *I*?" He glared at Biscane and pointed at him. "You took on a crazy gunman, and you're asking if I'm okay?" Then Jory strode across the distance separating them and pulled Biscane into a tight hug. "Goddamnit, don't ever scare me like that again."

Sighing, Biscane clutched his mate close to his chest. "I'm fine, too," he whispered into Jory's ear while rubbing up and down his back. "And I'd never let anything happen to you." Biscane threaded his fingers into Jory's short hair, still finding it damp from their earlier shower, and used the hold to force his mate's head back. When Jory met his gaze, Biscane smiled down at him. "You are my mate, my love, the other half of my soul. I'll always keep you safe." Biscane glanced down at his human form. "No matter what I look like."

Jory's tension eased under Biscane's continued touches. "God, I was so scared for you."

Biscane shook his head. After a glance at George, finding him still out, he whispered, "Only a head or heart shot would have killed me, Jory, and he's not a good enough marksman to do that." With a wink, he murmured, "Everything else, I'll heal from within a few weeks." Then Biscane took the opportunity to remind, "You will, too, although I never want to see *you* shot."

Scowling at Biscane, Jory stated, "I don't want you to have

to heal from that either."

While understanding, Biscane had to remind, "I'm an enforcer for an elder. There are times where I *will* have to fight." Hoping to soften that admonishment, he added, "But now that I have you waiting for me to finish my shift, I'll always strive to return to you safe and healthy."

Jory held Biscane's gaze for several long seconds, searching his gaze. Then his shoulders sagged as his tension eased from him. "I guess that's the best I could possibly hope from any partner." With a slight smile, he added, "After all, one of us could get plevvied by a runaway semi while crossing the street."

Biscane growled as he narrowed his eyes at Jory. "That is *not* a pleasant thought."

Rolling his eyes, Jory told him, "What I'm saying is that we never know how much time we have on this earth. Even with the safest job in the world, we should appreciate every moment we have with our family, friends, and those we love." Then Jory whispered, "And I love you, too."

Biscane felt those words all the way to his heart. Grinning broadly, he tucked his nose into the crook of Jory's neck and inhaled deeply. He relished the scent of his healthy mate while reveling in having him safe in his arms.

"My mate," Biscane whispered while pressing gentle kisses to his mate's neck. "All mine."

"All yours."

As much as Biscane would have loved to take Jory to his bedroom and worship every inch of his body all over again, the sound of George moaning softly reminded him of his duty. He eased his hold on Jory and peered at the downed human. Seeing his eyelashes begin to flutter, he released Jory.

"Got any zip ties or rope?" Biscane asked as he eyed their slowly rousing attacker. When he realized Jory appeared to be thinking hard, he chuckled. "How about a few ties you don't like?"

Jory appeared relieved as he nodded and hustled from the room. In less than twenty seconds, he returned with a half-dozen ties . . . and they were all brightly colored with a Christmas theme.

Biscane took them and quickly used them to truss George's arms behind his back and his legs together. Using another, he shoved it into his mouth as a gag. He straightened and held up another tie, peering at the myriad of *Dr. Seuss Grinches* all over it.

"Not a fan of Christmas?" Biscane asked curiously. In his experience, most humans loved the holiday.

"Meh." Jory waggled his hand in a so-so gesture. "I don't have a problem with it," he told him. "But can you see me wearing one of those to court?"

Biscane nodded. "Point taken." Then he touched Jory's shoulder. "I'm getting my phone. Be right back, and don't go near him."

Jory lifted his hands and claimed, "I'm going to get a cup of coffee. Want one?"

Remembering the last cup of coffee he'd had, Biscane grimaced. "Do you have any black tea?" He decided it was time to switch. There were other ways to get caffeine.

Chuckling, Jory nodded. "I think I do."

Once Jory was headed to the kitchen, Biscane jogged to the bedroom. He tracked down his phone and, as he returned to the living room, dialed Elder Bodb's number.

"Hello, Biscane," the elder greeted. "I suppose congratulations are in order if you're calling me at this time of day."

Grinning broadly, Biscane couldn't contain his pleasure as he replied, "Yep. The bond is complete."

"I'm very happy for you, my old friend," Bodb stated, and his pleasure was clear in his tone. "I suppose I may be losing you to the city for a few years."

Biscane grimaced, then admitted, "Probably, although we haven't discussed that yet." Then, recalling a comment Jory had made in passing, he added, "Although, Jory did say he was getting me a key to his condo."

Bodb's deep chuckles came through the line. "Well, then. There you go." After a pause, he asked, "Are you calling to tell me that you need leave from your schedule for a few more days? Because we already have you off for the next week."

"Actually, I'm calling for help," Biscane told his elder. "Attain's father, George Walsh, dropped by Jory's condo. He admitted to bribing LeeAnn to get Attain alone and off the ranch, then to killing her when she failed." He grimaced. While he hadn't ended up liking the woman, he hadn't wanted that end for her. "On top of that, George has been driving anyone who doesn't meet his criteria for . . . living their life . . . out of the firm. I'm still a little confused on how he decided who was fit to stay and who wasn't," Biscane admitted. "Maybe no one would understand but him, since he seemed quite unhinged when he began waving his gun around before I disarmed him."

"Gods," Bodb grumbled. "I should have known that asshole wouldn't be able to accept the loss of control over his son." After another deep sigh, Bodb told him, "I'll call Archer and give him a heads up. I believe Spieron's brother, Sandro, is on duty right now. Even though you're in the city's jurisdiction, the murder took place in the Archer's. We'll have George brought under our purview in no time."

"Got it," Biscane replied, understanding perfectly. They would be using the human laws for this issue. "I'll call nine-one-one now."

"Use Jory's phone," Bodb ordered. "Seeing as it's his coworker and phone call times could look odd."

"Will do," Biscane replied. After hanging up, he called, "Jory, where's your phone?"

"Bedroom nightstand," Jory called back.

Biscane made a quick check of the ties binding George, then retrieved his mate's phone. As he relayed the information to the dispatcher, he returned to the front room. He found Jory sitting at the dining room table, staring at a glaring George.

Crossing to the table, Biscane settled next to his mate. He leaned over and pecked a kiss to his lover's lips. Then he took the cup of tea, smiling in appreciation.

"I'm sorry this came down on you," Jory murmured softly.

"What do you mean?" Biscane asked curiously before taking a sip of the tea.

Not bad.

Jory sighed and shook his head, frowning at George. "He said he's been driving off everyone who he doesn't think matches his ideals," he pointed out. Then he focused on Biscane with a frustrated look. "Ten to one says he's the person deleting files and making others look bad."

"If he is, we'll figure out a way to pin that on him," Biscane assured, still uncertain what Jory was driving at.

Shaking his head, Jory told him, "If George hadn't done that, then I never would have ended up at the ranch that night. I was there asking for clarification on a file from Attain."

Biscane grinned broadly, which he knew surprised Jory. "Ah," he mused. "Then we should thank him."

"Huh?"

Chuckling, Biscane put down his mug and eased closer to his mate. "Well, without his meddling" — he rested his hands on Jory's hips and pulled him closer — "we never would have met."

Jory stared at him wide-eyed for a second. Then he grinned. "You're absolutely right." A wicked gleam entered his mate's eyes, and he raised his voice, calling, "Thanks, George. Without you, I never would have met Biscane."

As George started a muffled string of noises that were probably profanities, Biscane laughed and pulled Jory onto his lap. By his calculations, they had several minutes before a cop arrived, and he had every intention of spending the time by making out with his mate.

Convinced it was a damn fine idea, Biscane did just that.

You may also enjoy the following from eXtasy Books Inc:

Snorkeling with a Sawshark
Charlie Richards

Excerpt

Westram McKinley strolled slowly through his assigned section of the World of Aquatica marine park. While his gaze strayed over everything around him, his mind wasn't on his job. It was a good thing just the presence of a man in a security uniform dissuaded most from doing anything, because Westram would surely have missed anyone actually doing wrongdoing.

Instead, just as it had been for the last couple of months, Westram's mind was firmly fixed on his mate—Noah Redruvian. He longed to pull the sweet-smelling and cute-as-hell human into his arms. He wanted to taste his full lips and squeeze his plump ass.

Too bad Westram didn't see that happening anytime soon.

All because of one thoughtless comment.

When Westram had first met Noah, he'd been there in a guard capacity. A stalker had been after Arthur, his alpha's mate. They'd chosen a plan to lure the man out. That created danger for Arthur's friends, too.

Westram had been assigned to Noah, while Dare — a fellow shifter enforcer — had been ordered to watch Arthur's other best friend, Jacob. Walking into the house where the pair waited — Arthur had wanted to explain the situation first — had been the most surreal and magical moment of Westram's nearly two century life.

Then Jacob had opened his big mouth, starting a chain reaction that caused Westram to mentally cringe any time he thought about it.

"Mmm," Jacob had purred, eyeing Dare like a tasty steak. "If you're gonna be my body guard, big guy, I guess I don't have a problem with it." Jacob had extended his hand to him.

Dare had grinned broadly as he'd reached out and wrapped his large dark hand around Jacob's much smaller one. Using the hold, he'd tugged the human close while saying, "Does that mean you'd be amenable to recreating a scene or two from The Bodyguard?"

Resting his free hand on Dare's chest, Jacob grinned up at him, obvious heat in his green eyes. "Oh, definitely."

Growling softly, Dare lowered his head, placing his lips close to Jacob's ear. "I look forward to that."

Westram would forever deny his behavior on the pheromones the pair were pumping out.

Fixing his gaze on Noah, Westram had skimmed the backs of his forefingers down his arm. "What about you, handsome?" he asked, his voice husky with need. Reaching Noah's hand, he slid his fingers around the human's much smaller ones. "Are you into role play, too?"

In truth, Westram wouldn't have cared either way. Noah was his mate. He would happily take him any way he could get him.

Noah had yanked his hand away from Westram. "No," he stated flatly. With a scowl, he crossed his arms and curled his hands into fists. "I'm not. Nor do I care for one night stands, flings, or getting my rocks off with any piece of ass who hits on me."

Westram opened his mouth, intending to apologize, but Noah turned away from him and addressed Arthur. "I hope this plan works fast," he stated. "I don't need some bruiser who thinks only with his dick dogging my steps."

"Westram does know how to be a gentleman," Alpha Kaiser claimed reassuringly.

When Noah scoffed and moved toward the table, perhaps to retrieve one of the beers sitting on it, Kaiser turned his attention back to Westram and arched one brow in silent question.

Wincing for just an instant, Westram cut his gaze toward Noah, then refocused on his alpha.

Alpha Kaiser narrowed his eyes, but since neither Noah or Jacob knew about shifters—and they didn't plan to tell them unless absolutely necessary—not much could be said . . . yet.

"How are you doing?"

Westram didn't quite manage to hide his jerk of surprise upon hearing Beta William's softly spoken question.

Meeting William's understanding gaze, Westram opened his mouth, then closed it again. He rubbed at his chest, his heart sending phantom pains through him at being separated from his mate. Instead of answering, Westram just shook his head.

William nodded. "Yeah, I sorta thought that when I saw the vacant glint in your eyes." Resting his hand on Westram's nape, he squeezed supportively. "Do you need a break to compose yourself?"

Bowing his head a little, Westram admitted, "I don't know if that will help." Grimacing, he told the beta, "My shark is pushing me to jump into the ocean so he can swim down to San Diego and we can track Noah down." Upon seeing the concerned glint enter William's green eyes, Westram quickly added, "I know that's not a possibility. My mate doesn't want to see me, but the only way I can swim these days is with you or Kaiser are near."

Having met Noah Redruvian months before, Westram's

longnosed saw-shark was becoming damn pushy. His animal didn't understand the problem. He wanted Westram to grab the man, toss him into the ocean, and let the shark drag him home — literally.

So not an option.

Alpha Kaiser and his brother, William, were both huge squid — although not the same kind — and could keep his shark from taking off.

William nodded, squeezed his neck once more, then released him. "Well, take five anyway. Arthur wants to talk to you."

Confused, even as Westram nodded, he commented, "I thought he was in video conferences all day."

"He was supposed to," William confirmed, shoving his hands into his pockets. "So it must be something important for him to step out for a few minutes and text me to get you."

Westram nodded. "I'll hurry over there." Then he started speed walking in the direction that would take him out of the north gate of the park. The narrow paved road led to a sprawling complex of condominiums. Most of the people working at the park lived there. Many were shifters with a smattering of human mates thrown in.

In Kaiser's suite, he'd set up a massive office for Arthur to work remotely from. The human owned an engineering business out of San Diego. On the occasions he couldn't do something from their location north of Sacramento, Kaiser would fly there with Arthur on a private jet.

Westram knew Noah worked as an accountant, so he would be able to work from anywhere, too. He had even already moved into a larger suite and fitted one of the rooms as an elaborate home office. Westram just had to figure out how to convince Noah that he was sincere.

Except, how can I do that when he won't even take my calls?

Arthur told Westram to be patient. He was putting a good

word in for him, but it would take time. Evidently, his ex-boyfriend had been a cheating bastard who'd mentally abused Noah. The man needed time to heal before accepting the fact that Westram wasn't just like him.

Westram wished he could help Noah heal, but his beautiful mate wasn't ready to accept his advances, yet.

Someday.

That was the only promise he could make to his shark.

We have time. We're only a little over two hundred years old. We'll have centuries together, once Noah is ready.

Those were the thoughts Westram clung to when he lay down to sleep at night with loneliness causing his gut to clench and his arms aching to hold his human and soothe away all his fears.

Once Westram was out of the marine park, he broke into a sprint. He streaked up the path as fast as his legs would carry him. Being a shifter, that was pretty quickly, so it only took him a couple of minutes to reach Kaiser and Arthur's apartment.

Westram's knock on the door was immediately answered by Arthur. The human wore a headset and he was speaking into it. At the same time, he beckoned Westram into the room.

"Yes, George," Arthur was saying. "I apologize, but I need that five minute break now." A smile creased his lips as he chuckled softly. "I'm glad the restroom break is welcomed. I'm putting the call on hold and I'll be back in five."

Then Arthur hit a button on the left side of the earpiece. He took the device off his head and set it on the coffee table. Turning away, he began to pace while scrubbing his fingers through his hair.

Seeing the alpha-mate's tension, Westram shifted uneasily. "If there's anything I can do to help," he began, hoping the human would confide in him.

"I know, Westram," Arthur replied immediately, turning to face him. "I called you because it's about Noah."

Westram's gut clenched. "Noah?" Seeing the grimace on

Arthur's face, he hated the bad feeling that burst through him. "What's wrong with Noah?"

Arthur shrugged, his expression appearing helpless. "I'm not sure. That's the problem."

The butterflies in his stomach morphed into bile in his throat. "What do you mean?"

"He hasn't responded to my calls or texts in two days," Arthur told him. "That's never happened before. He's always prompt." Running his hands through his hair again, Arthur continued, "I'd go see him, but I have three days of meetings I just can't reschedule. I—""

"I'll go," Westram cut in. "Whether he wants to see me or not, I'll see what's going on."

Sighing with obvious relief, Arthur nodded. "I thought you'd say that. I have the jet being readied at the airport." After a second of hesitation, he added, "Maybe take Doc Keller and Solomon with you?"

Westram growled as his uneasiness turned to a feral need to see his mate safe and healthy. "You think there was trouble?"

Arthur shook his head. "I sure as hell hope not, but he made an odd comment the last time I spoke with him. Something about feeling as if he was being watched." Frowning, Arthur told him, "When I questioned him about it, Noah laughed it off and said he was just being paranoid. Then he changed the subject."

Turning toward the door, Westram claimed, "I'm on it."

No matter what, Westram would make certain his mate was safe, even if he had to endure some yelling from the man to do it.

About the Author

Charlie started writing fantasy when she was eight, and after stumbling onto her first erotic romance at age nineteen, she realized her true calling. She now focuses on writing gay erotic romance, normally of the paranormal variety, with heroes of all kinds. With the help and support of her husband, Charlie finally fulfilled one of her life-long goals . . . move to acreage with her horses. You can often find her curled up with her laptop and a cup of tea or glass of wine, creating her next adventure. Charlie enjoys exploring the mountains of her new Oregon home on horseback, 4-wheeler, or motorcycle.

She can be reached at ch.richards2010@yahoo.com

Or visit her at www.charlie-richards.com